MY LiFe
as
Invisible
Intestines

BOOKS BY BILL MYERS

The Incredible Worlds of Wally McDoogle (20 books):

—*My Life As a Smashed Burrito with Extra Hot Sauce*
—*My Life As Alien Monster Bait*
—*My Life As a Broken Bungee Cord*
—*My Life As Crocodile Junk Food*
—*My Life As Dinosaur Dental Floss*
—*My Life As a Torpedo Test Target*
—*My Life As a Human Hockey Puck*
—*My Life As an Afterthought Astronaut*
—*My Life As Reindeer Road Kill*
—*My Life As a Toasted Time Traveler*
—*My Life As Polluted Pond Scum*
—*My Life As a Bigfoot Breath Mint*
—*My Life As a Blundering Ballerina*
—*My Life As a Screaming Skydiver*
—*My Life As a Human Hairball*
—*My Life As a Walrus Whoopee Cushion*
—*My Life As a Mixed-Up Millennium Bug*
—*My Life As a Beat-Up Basketball Backboard*
—*My Life As a Cowboy Cowpie*
—*My Life As Invisible Intestines with Intense Indigestion*

Other Series:

McGee and Me! (12 books)

Bloodhounds, Inc. (10 books)

Forbidden Doors (10 books)

Teen Nonfiction

Hot Topics, Tough Questions
Faith Encounter
Just Believe It

Picture Book

Baseball for Breakfast

www.Billmyers.com

MY LiFe as

Invisible Intestines

with intense indigestion

BILL MYERS

Tommy NELSON®

Thomas Nelson, Inc.
Nashville

MY LIFE AS INVISIBLE INTESTINES WITH INTENSE INDIGESTION

Published in Nashville, Tennessee, by Tommy Nelson®, a division of Thomas Nelson, Inc. Visit us on the Web at www.tommynelson.com.

Scripture quotations marked (NIV) are from the *Holy Bible, New International Version*. Copyright © 1973, 1978, 1984 International Bible Society. Used by permission of Zondervan Bible Publishers.

Library of Congress Cataloging-in-Publication Data

Myers, Bill, 1953–
    My Life as invisible intestines (with intense indigestion) / Bill Myers.
        p. cm.—(The incredible worlds of Wally McDoogle ; #20)
    Summary: Wally McDoogle, young writer of superhero stories, has a series of misadventures when Wall Street and Opera decide he should use his sudden invisibility to make money and have fun.
    ISBN 0-8499-5991-8
    [1. Cheating—Fiction. 2. Christian life—Fiction. 3. Humorous stories.] I. Title.
PZ7.M98234 Myse2001
[Fic]—dc21

                                                        2001042579

Printed in the United States of America

01 02 03 04 05 PHX 5 4 3 2

For all the cool folks
at Young Writer's Institute . . .

Thanks for letting me play.

"Whoever can be trusted with very little can also be trusted with much, and whoever is dishonest with very little will also be dishonest with much. So if you have not been trustworthy in handling worldly wealth, who will trust you with true riches?"

—Luke 16:10–11 (NIV)

Contents

Chapter 1

Just for Starters . . .

The interesting thing about cheating is a ton of people do it. From presidents to priests, from young kids to old codgers, from famous movie stars to mass murderers. And, speaking from personal experience, I've gotta tell you it's kinda fun, it's kinda cool, and

IT'S THE STUPIDEST THING I'VE EVER DONE IN MY LIFE!
(Oh, sorry, didn't mean to yell.
Guess I'm sort of touchy about the subject right now.)

BUT FOR GOOD REASON!
(sorry . . .)

It all started innocently enough. (Isn't that how all my disasters start?) Just another one of our lame field trips to another lame science laboratory courtesy of our lame science teacher, Mr. Reptenson. Don't get me wrong, I've got nothing against scientists, I know we need somebody to sell all those calculators and pocket protectors to . . . and I appreciate the sleep I've been able to catch up on in Mr. Reptenson's class. But, let's face it, science and I haven't been like the best of friends.

First there was my little science fair project on raising fleas that got out of control in *My Life As Alien Monster Bait* (nothing a few thousand flea collars couldn't fix)—and my accidental journey on the Space Shuttle in *Afterthought Astronaut* (at least they let me ride inside . . . most of the time)—and my little adventure skipping through time as a *Toasted Time Traveler* (any idea how long it takes to get dinosaur drool out of your hair?).

And now, to make matters worse, we were in exactly the same laboratory where Wall Street (my best friend, even if she is a girl) and I got ourselves shrunk down and accidentally swallowed in *My Life As a Human Hairball*.

(Hey, everybody needs a hobby—mine just happens to be trying to survive life.)

The good news was, we had a different tour

guide than the last time. (I guess they're only allowed so many nervous breakdowns per year.) The bad news was, science was still science and Wally McDoogle was still . . . well, you get the picture.

"What's that big contraption for?" Opera, my other best friend, asked the guide. As a human eating machine, Opera was cramming another handful of Chippy Chipper potato chips into his mouth. He was always cramming handfuls of Chippy Chipper potato chips into his mouth . . . when he wasn't cramming in handfuls of candy, cakes, or cookies. Yes sir, if it started with the letter "C" my pal was cramming it. Unless, of course, it came to carrots, celery, or cauliflower —after all, everyone has his limit.

The guide smiled proudly at the towering machine beside her. "This is our Optical Oscillating Proton Positioning System," she said.

"Your, *BURP,* what?" Opera asked.

The guide's smile wilted slightly. "We call it 'OOPS' for short," she said. "When we get all the bugs worked out, it will rearrange the protons of any given object to fit the precise molecular specifications of another."

"Oh, of, *BELCH,* course," Opera nodded.

The smile wilted some more. She turned to the rest of the group. "If you place an apple under the OOPS beam and enter the word 'lemon' into the keyboard . . . the beam coming from the machine will rearrange the molecular structure of the apple and turn it into a lemon. The atoms will be the same, they'll just be rearranged."

"Cool," Wall Street said. I threw my friend a glance. Of course, her mind was already starting to turn—which, of course, made me a little nervous. "So," she asked, "if I were to, like, put a piece of paper under the beam and type in 'A THOUSAND-DOLLAR BILL,' it would change my paper into a thousand-dollar bill?" (Wall Street has a tiny little thing about money.)

The tour guide answered, "I suppose that's a possibility."

Wall Street grew more excited. "Or if I put a rock under it and typed in 'WORLD'S MOST EXPENSIVE DIAMOND' I could create a diamond worth a billion dollars?!" (Actually, Wall Street has a *BIG* thing about money.)

"Perhaps, but—"

"Or if I . . . if I . . ." (By now my pal was getting herself so worked up she could barely speak.) ". . . if I said to turn a ton of garbage into a ton of gold I'd be a millionaire overnight?!"

"Yes, well, I suppose," the guide answered nervously, "but we intend to put the OOPS to far more noble purposes than that." Eager to change the subject, she started toward the next room. "Now, if you will all follow me to our next lab, I think you'll find our discussion on the genetic structure of the South American fruit fly extremely exhilarating."

The rest of the class began following her, but Wall Street had worked herself up into such a pitch that she had to lean against the wall to catch her breath.

"Are you okay?" I asked.

"Okay?" she gasped. "*Okay?!*"

"Hey, take it easy," I said.

"Take it easy?! Wally, don't you get it? I could become a millionaire in just a few seconds. Forget a millionaire, make that a gazillionaire! So could you. All we have to do is turn on that machine and a minute later walk out of here with more money than we could carry."

"Or more, *munch, munch,* chips than we could eat," Opera added from beside me.

I turned to him. "What do you mean?"

"It doesn't have to be money, we can create anything including these, *burp,* chips. Just imagine bags and bags of these grease-saturated, salt-coated, artery-plugging delicacies . . ." He was smacking his lips and getting a dreamy look on his face.

"But . . . isn't that like stealing or something?" I asked.

"What are we stealing?" Wall Street said.

"I'm not sure—but making money from nothing, or creating bags of somebody else's potato chips—somehow it feels like we're cheating."

"Who cares?" Wall Street argued. "It's not like anybody's getting hurt."

"Burp." Opera nodded in agreement.

"Yeah," I said, "but still—"

K-Bang

We spun around to see that the door to the lab had just closed. The last of our class had left, and now we were all alone with OOPS. Just the three of us—Wall Street's greed, Opera's hunger . . . and my uneasy conscience.

"Guys . . ."

"Not now, Wally." Wall Street was already at OOPS's side switching switches, dialing dials, and knobbing knobs. It was the usual high-tech, multibillion-dollar machine with more flashing lights than the cop car that pulled Dad over for speeding.

"How do you know what you're doing?" I asked.

"No sweat." She grinned. "I'm just turning every button that says 'OFF' to 'ON.'"

"Makes sense to me," Opera belched.

"Guys . . ."

"So, who has a piece of paper?" Wall Street asked. "Let's get this puppy running and start making some cold, hard cash!"

We all reached into our pockets, but none of us had any paper. The best we came up with was a shiny penny and a lint-covered Sugar Bomb from my pockets; a dozen empty Chippy Chipper wrappers from Opera's pockets; and the usual stocks, junk bonds, and money market accounts from Wall Street's.

"Guess we'll have to come back another time," I said hopefully.

"Not so fast," Wall Street replied. "Let's see what we can get out of your penny."

"Wall Street . . . ," I whined.

"Go ahead," she said. "Put it on that platform under the beam. Let's see if we can turn it into a hundred-dollar gold piece or something. Go ahead."

Reluctantly, I set the penny on the platform.

"Okay," Wall Street said. "Stand back."

We all took a healthy step backward.

She reached for the biggest and brightest of all the buttons, the one labeled: *OOPS ACTIVATION.*

"Here goes nothing," she said.

"I hope you're right," I muttered.

She pressed the button.

The lights in the laboratory dimmed slightly. The OOPS gave a low rumble that quickly turned into a high whine.

"It's, *burp,* happening!" Opera yelled. "It's, *belch,* working!"

Suddenly, a tiny red beam shot out and struck the new penny. That was the good news. The bad news was, the beam bounced off Abe Lincoln's shiny new forehead and shot out in another direction. Another direction that just happened to be where I was standing.

K-ZAPP!

"AUGH!" I screamed, grabbing my eyes. "I can't see, I can't see!"

"Turn it off!" Opera yelled. "Turn it off!"

Immediately, Wall Street reached over and shut down OOPS. The surrounding lights came back up as the machine quickly whined down. After a moment or two I could finally see again.

"Wally, are you okay?" Wall Street asked. "Are you all right?"

I gave myself a quick once-over and was surprised to see that nothing was damaged. How odd. Could I have really gotten off that easily? (Of course, we all know better, but play along with me for these next few pages just for fun.)

"Yeah, I think so," I finally said. "Yeah, I'm fine."

We all turned to the penny. Nothing had happened to it, either. Nothing at all.

"I don't get it," Wall Street said, taking a step closer. "We turned on the machine, the beam struck the penny, but—" Suddenly, she struck her forehead. "Of course." She pointed to the computer screen, which was completely empty. "I forgot to type in what we wanted it to become."

We all nodded in agreement.

Without a word she headed for the keyboard. But she barely started to type before the door to the lab flew open and two security police stormed in. Two security police who looked anything but happy.

"What are you kids doing?" they demanded. But before Wall Street could make up a suitable lie, they ordered, "You come with us! Come with us immediately."

Reluctantly we followed. (Not, of course, before Wall Street reached out to scoop up the penny from the platform—hey, a penny saved is another penny closer to making her first million.)

Not exactly treating us like delicate china, the guards quickly escorted us to face the tour guide and Mr. Reptenson. After that, of course, would come facing our folks and some sort of punishment. But that was okay. To be honest, part of me was relieved. A *BIG* part of me. Because for the first time that I could remember, nothing bad had happened. I mean, other than losing a penny and probably being grounded for a few weeks, everything was okay—no crazy chaos, no mass destruction, no breaking or rearranging of Wally body parts. It was unbelievable, like a dream come true.

Unfortunately, we all know about my dreams. They always become nightmares. . . .

Chapter 2

"Uh-Oh..."

After all the lectures from our tour guide, Mr. Reptenson, Mom, Dad, and anybody else who felt like yelling, I was finally (and mercifully) sent to my room. Then, doing what I always do when there's nothing to do, I whipped out Ol' Betsy, my laptop computer. I climbed into bed without even wasting time to take off my clothes and started another one of my stories. Yes sir, nothing like drowning your sorrows in a good dose of superheroism. . . .

"MuperMlob, melp me! Melp me, Mu-perMlob!"

The sensationally sloppy SuperSlob looks up from his morning breakfast—a tasty mixture of last week's lima bean casserole and cold, leftover

pizza (covered in hardened grease,
of course), smothered in frozen orange
juice so old and moldy that it should
be called "fuzzy-green juice." All of
which is dumped together into
a blender to create a rich, pasty
goo the color of a toxic waste site—
which, come to think about it, is
about how it tastes. (Hey, the guy's
a superhero, not a supergourmet.)

"MuperMlob, melp me, melp me!"

There it is again, that voice. It's
coming from upstairs. And, whoever it
is, it sounds like she's in trouble.

Instantly, SuperSlob leaps from
his plastic lawn chair (which he uses
as a sofa in the living room since
it's much easier to hose down) and
races up the stairs doing his best
not to trip over the hundreds of
half-empty Domino's Pizza boxes, broken CD cases, and discarded Happy
Meal toys. (And you thought he got
his name by accident?)

"MuperMlob!" It's coming from his
bedroom. "MuperMlob! MuperMlob!" The
voice sounds strangely familiar...
and for good reason.

"Mom," he cries, "is that you?"

"Melp me, MuperMlob, melp me!"

He arrives at his bedroom door and discovers to his horror that his mom has actually tried to enter the room.

"MuperMlob! MuperMlob!"

Without a moment's hesitation, he leaps into action and climbs over the towering mountain of dirty socks, dirty shirts, dirty underwear, and dirty anything else he has ever worn in his life. (Hey, it's either that or actually having to wash them, which, as you might have guessed, isn't exactly his style.)

"Melp me, MuperMlob, melp me!"

Utilizing every muscle of his muscular manliness, he reaches the summit of Mount McSloby. Now he begins digging and burrowing his way down. Nothing will *(dig, dig, burrow, burrow)* stop him. No amount of discarded comic books, no number of used printer ink cartridges, not even the 3,071 empty cans of Dr Pepper (diet, of course—hey, even a slob needs to keep his neat and trim superhero figure).

At last he sees his mother's hand
sticking up through the mess, and
with a little more *dig, dig, digging*
and a lot more *burrow, burrow, burrowing,* he is finally able to pull
her from the debris.

Throwing her arms around him, she
cries, "Oh, MuperMlob, MuperMlob."

"Mom"——he glances around embar-
rassed——"you can talk normal now. Your
mouth is no longer buried in junk."

"Yes, of course," she cries as she
once again throws her arms around him.
"Oh, SuperSlob!"

After letting her do her mom thing
another moment, he finally pries her
off and asks, "What were you doing
trying to come in here? You weren't
actually thinking of cleaning, were
you?"

"Oh, no, Dear," she says, "I know
better than that."

"Or making my bed?"

"I wouldn't even know where to
find it."

"Then what were you risking your
life coming in here for?"

"A SuperSlob fax just came in,"

she says, producing a piece of grease-stained paper. "I was bringing it up to you."

"Who's it from?" our hero asks.

"The President."

"Oh, no! Again?" Our hero sighs. He reaches for the paper and begins reading it through the globs of lima bean casserole, cold pizza, and fuzzy-green juice dripping from his hands. Immediately, he notices that every sentence is written in perfect handwriting. The staggering neatness sends a pain shooting through his brain. "What's going on?" he cries. "I begged him never to send messages this tidy."

"I know!" his mother exclaims. "Look how neat the letters are, how straight the margins are."

The pain fills our hero's brain. "Is there no end to his cruelty?" He gasps.

"And to top it off, I don't see a single misspelled word!"

"Oh, Mom...you don't suppose——"

Ta-Da-DAAAA

(He's interrupted by the scary music that always plays when the bad guy is introduced.)

"I'm afraid you're right, Dear," his mom says. "It looks like the world is once again being attacked by—"

Ta-Da-DAAAA

(The real bad guys get two blasts of scary music.)

"...Neat Freak."

As they stand in the room, a most amazing thing begins to happen. As if by magic, all of the clothes in Super-Slob's room begin moving by themselves. Shirts mysteriously move toward hangers to be hung up. Pants begin folding themselves. Even the socks begin sorting themselves and, horror of horrors, actually turning themselves right side out.

What is going on? What sinister plan is Neat Freak pulling off this time? And more important, why is a sloppy person the hero of our story and a neat guy the villain? Does the writer really think he can get away with such mixed-up morality? Does he really think Mom or Dad or Grandma will actually buy you such a book? (Oh, never mind, guess they have.) And, suddenly, just when things are at their neatest—

"Lights out, loser."

I glanced up to see my older brother Burt (or was it Brock? I can never keep those twins straight) sneering at me from my doorway. Burt (or was it Brock?) was always sneering at me—when he wasn't ridiculing me, making fun of me, or damaging my emotional health in some other way. Ah, big brothers, what thoughtful, sensitive creatures.

And as the younger brother, my responsibility was to respond to him with equal compassion. "Who died and made you head Neanderthal?"

He scratched his head, obviously not understanding the word 'Neanderthal.' Hey, he's only been in the eleventh grade two years. Finally he spoke. "Mom and Dad are already in bed.

They're headin' out early tomorrow for their trip."

"Meaning?" I asked, fearing the worst.

"Meaning me and Burt are in charge for the next three days." He cranked up one of his more sinister grins. "Meaning you have to do whatever we say whenever we say it."

Great, I thought, *just great. What else could go wrong?* Little did I realize when I turned out the light and went to sleep that something a lot wronger than this wrong was already working its wrongness.

Translation: Buckle in folks.
It's going to get a lot worse.

* * * * *

As weird as it sounds, when I woke up the next morning I didn't realize I'd turned invisible. (Unlike you, I didn't have this book's title to clue me in . . . though I bet you're still wondering about the "intestine" stuff, aren't you? Relax, we'll get to it, we'll get to it, unfortunately, we'll get to it.)

Now, where was I? Oh, yeah. I really didn't know I'd turned invisible until I was outside and heading for school. (Burt and Brock always treat me like I don't exist, so being ignored by them was nothing unusual. And my little sister, Carrie, spends every waking hour hogging the bathroom mirror, so it's not like I could catch my reflection or anything.) In fact, it wasn't until I had joined Wall Street and Opera on the way to school that I even noticed there was a problem.

"Hey, guys," I called.

"Hey," they answered without looking up. Wall Street was deep in conversation, and Opera was deep in, well, potato chip consumption. After all, it had been nearly twenty minutes since he'd eaten breakfast.

She continued their conversation. "I mean, I put it there on the dresser when I went to bed. When I woke up this morning, it's like it had completely vanished."

"Don't, *munch, munch,* sweat it," Opera said. "It's just a penny."

Wall Street turned to him in shock. "Just a penny? Just a penny!? Do you realize how many pennies make up a dollar?"

"Uh, *crunch*, er, *munch,* . . ." High finances have never been one of Opera's strengths.

"Or how many dollars it takes to make a million?"

"Duh, *burp,* . . ." Okay, neither has math.

"Maybe you just misplaced it," I offered. But I knew my mistake before I'd even finished the sentence. Wall Street misplacing money would be like the state of Florida miscounting presidential ballots. Okay, bad example. It would be like people actually liking Teletubbies. Okay, another bad example. It would be like—

"Don't be stupid," she said, turning to me. "When was the last time I ever misplaced—" Suddenly, she stopped. "Hey, where'd you go?"

I frowned. "What?"

"Wally?" She began looking all around, acting like she didn't see me. "Wally, where are you?"

"I'm right here."

Opera glanced up from his bag of chips. "Wally?" he called. "Wally?" Then, turning to Wall Street he said, "He was here a minute ago. I just heard him."

"Guys," I said. "What are you doing?"

They exchanged glances. Finally, Wall Street broke into a grin. "Okay, McDoogle . . ." She looked to the bushes behind me, then over to the nearby trees. "How are you pulling this off?" she asked. "Loudspeakers, is that it? You got some sort of wireless microphone and PA system?"

"What are you talking about?" I asked.

"Wow," Opera said, so impressed that he'd

even stopped chewing. "You're good. Real, *burp,* good." (He stopped chewing but not burping.)

"Guys?" I said.

Still grinning, Wall Street stuck her hand out in my direction. Well, actually, not in my direction. More like in my

"OW!"

"That's my eye!" I cried.

She immediately pulled back her hand. "Wally?"

"What?" I said, rubbing my eye with my hand. Well, it was supposed to be my hand. But as I looked I noticed I was busy rubbing my eye with thin air.

Thin air?! (Sorry, I'm shouting again.) But how was that possible?! Unfortunately, it wasn't just my hand that was missing. I also noticed that the arm attached to my hand was gone. Come to think of it, so was my other hand and my other arm and my other . . . all of me!!

"Yikes!!" I cried. "What's going on?!?"

But Wall Street just kept on grinning. "Oh, this is slick," she said with a knowing nod. "Very, very slick."

"Slick nothing!" I screamed. "This is impossible!"

Now Opera began to nod and grin. "He's good,

real good. But where are you really, Wally?" he asked, glancing around.

"I'm right here!" I shouted.

"Right where?"

"Right here in front of you!"

"Yeah, right." Wall Street snickered.

I don't know what was worse—the fact that they couldn't see me, or that they didn't understand the seriousness of my problem.

"Guys, I'm right here!" I yelled. "Right here in front of you!" I waved my hand in front of their faces. They didn't even blink. They just kept grinning broader and nodding bigger. "Guys," I shouted, "something terrible has happened!!"

Broader grins and bigger nods.

I didn't know what to do. In desperation, I reached out for Opera's bag of chips. I lifted it from his hands so it looked like it was floating in midair.

Wall Street grinned, still looking around. "This is very, very cool, Wally. You have any idea how much money we could make selling your idea to magicians?"

"How are you doing it?" Opera asked. "With wires? Mirrors?"

"Guys!" I cried. "Something's wrong with me. I can't see myself!"

"Join the crowd." Opera chuckled.

"No, I'm serious!" I shouted. "I'm . . . I'm . . ."

"What are you going to tell us now?" Wall Street smirked. "That you're invisible?"

I looked back at my hands . . . or at least where my hands were supposed to be. But there was nothing. Just thin air . . . thin air and the bag of floating chips. "Yes," I cried. "Yes, yes! I don't know how it happened, but somehow, I've turned invisible!"

This set off another ripple of chuckles as they continued looking around, trying to figure out how I was doing the trick.

"Look!" I said, reaching into the bag and pulling out a handful of chips. "Look! Could wires do this?"

Suddenly, there was a handful of chips floating in the air. And, ever so slowly, Wall Street's and Opera's smiles began to fade.

"Can mirrors do this?" I demanded, cramming the chips into my mouth and starting to chew.

If they'd stopped smiling before, they stopped blinking now. Instead, they just stood and stared, their jaws dropping to the ground. But I wasn't done with my little demonstration.

"Or how 'bout this!" I shouted. With a big gulp I swallowed the mouthful of chips I'd been chewing.

Now they were no longer smiling, blinking . . . or breathing. And for good reason. I followed their stares down to my stomach and

"AUGHHH!"

shouted my head off (if I had a head to shout off). Because there, hanging in midair, in the middle of where I was supposed to be, floated the chewed-up chips. That's right. None of me was visible, not my clothes, not my body, not my stomach . . . only the food that had just now entered my stomach.

EEEEwwww. . . . Talk about gross. It was worse than dissecting frogs in science class, creepier than watching open-heart surgery on TV, more disgusting than trying to eat my sister's meat loaf (well, maybe not that bad, but close). In a flash, all three of us moved into action, each doing what we did best . . .

—Wall Street whipped off her coat and wrapped it around me so no one would see the floating lesson on potato chip digestion (either that or so no one would steal the idea before she could sell it).

—Opera reached out and yanked his bag of Chippy Chipper chips from my hands (the poor guy only had another four bags to get him through the rest of the day).

—And me, well, I don't remember all the details, but I do kinda remember closing my eyes, rocking back and forth a little, and finally passing out onto the sidewalk—not exactly dead, but not waking up for a while, either.

Chapter 3

Opera, the Good Luck Charm

"Hey, Dorkoid," a burly eighth-grade football player shouted at Opera. "Where's my water?"

"Coming!" Opera yelled. He raced onto the practice field with a bottle of water for the big bruiser.

"Hey, Wingnut!" another player shouted. "Grab me a towel!"

"Right away!" Opera yelled. He dashed to the sidelines to get a towel, then ran back onto the field with it.

I leaned over to Wall Street and whispered, "Why do we have to meet here? We'll never get anything accomplished."

She answered, "Coach Kilroy won't pass Opera in PE unless he does extra credit by helping the football team after school."

"I know that," I said. "But why do we have to meet now?"

"Hey, Jerkface!" a third bruiser yelled.

"Coming," Opera called.

Wall Street turned to where she thought I was standing and whispered, "The sooner we get going on my plan, the sooner we'll start making money."

Ah, yes, making money. No wonder she told me to keep quiet all day at school. No wonder she told me to just let the teachers mark me absent. She needed the time to figure out how to make a buck off my problem. Good ol' Wall Street.

gurgle . . . gurgle . . . gurgle . . .

"What's that?" she whispered.

"My stomach," I moaned, putting my hands where my stomach should be. But, of course, there was no stomach to be seen . . . come to think of it, there were no hands, either. "I haven't eaten anything since those chips this morning and I'm starved."

"Sorry, Wally," she sympathized. "But you saw what happens when you eat solid food."

"Yeah." I nodded. "Gross city."

gurgle . . . gurgle . . . gurgle . . .

Opera ran up to us, huffing and puffing.

"Okay," he gasped. "I think I've got a minute. Let's go over what we know."

"Right," Wall Street said. She reached into her pocket and pulled out something between her fingers.

"What's that?" Opera asked.

"My missing penny," she said. "I went home during lunch and grabbed it off my dresser."

Opera squinted. "I don't see anything."

"Exactly. Just like Wally, it's invisible." She took his hand and shoved the invisible penny into it.

"Hey, that's neat," he said, feeling and touching something none of us could see. "Very neat."

"So . . . ," Wall Street lowered her voice so she couldn't be heard. "First of all, we know that whatever happened to my penny is what happened to Wally."

I nodded. "We both got hit by that OOPS beam."

"Check. And so did your clothes, which is why we can't see them."

"Check."

"But why did OOPS make them invisible?" Opera asked, still feeling the penny. "I mean, we didn't type 'invisible' or anything on the computer."

"That's just it," Wall Street said. "We typed nothing on that computer, so . . . ," She let the

phrase hang in the air until one of us finally
got it.

"So . . . ," Opera shouted in understanding,
"Wally became nothing!"

"Shhh . . ." Wall Street motioned for him to
keep it down.

"Wonderful," I groaned, "I'm a nothing."

"Actually, you're something," she corrected
as my stomach gurgled some more.

"Yeah," I moaned, "invisible intestines."

"No"—she shook her head—"you're all there.
It's just that to everyone you *appear* to be nothing."

"That's supposed to make me feel better?"

"But why didn't it happen right away?"
Opera asked. "I mean, why did it take him all
night to get this way?"

"I'm not sure," Wall Street said. "Unless it
takes longer to realign atoms to make you look
like you're nothing."

"Hey, Opera, ol' buddy." We looked up to see
Jerry Bingham calling from the field. He's the
team's quarterback and a nice guy (even if he is
a superjock). "When you're done with your
friend, you want to grab me a drink?"

"Oh, sure," Opera shouted, starting toward
the cooler.

"No hurry," Jerry called. "Just when you get
the chance."

Opera nodded.

Wall Street continued her thinking. "So, the next question we have to ask ourselves is . . ."

"How to get me back to normal?" I asked.

"Not just yet," she answered. "I was figuring we should make some money off you first."

"Of course," I groaned. "What was I thinking?"

"Just for a little while," she said. "We don't know how long this will last, and we might as well take advantage of the situation while we can."

"Why am I not surprised?" I sighed.

"But how?" Opera asked.

"That's what I've been figuring," she said. "And I think I've got something. You know the old deserted house just down the street?"

"The Crider place?" I asked.

"Yeah. Well, what we do is start spreading rumors that the place is haunted. Then we start charging people admission to come see." She looked in the direction where she thought I stood. "And then you can start moving chairs and stuff and make them think the place really is haunted."

"Cool. . . ." Opera grinned.

"I don't know," I said. "Isn't that kinda like, you know, cheating or something?"

"Who will know? And if that OOPS beam wears off and you start getting visible again, we'll just tell them that the ghost moved out. But we gotta hurry. I can make up the fliers tonight, print them tomorrow, and we can start charging admission as early as tomorrow night."

"After the big game," Opera said.

"Sure." Wall Street nodded. "In fact, we can pass out the fliers during the game."

"Guys . . . ," I said. "I don't know if this is such a good idea. It's really not that honest and—"

"Hey, Idiot Boy," another bruiser shouted from the field. "Where's that water?!"

"Sorry," Opera said. He ran to the cooler, grabbed a couple of water bottles, then dashed out onto the field with them. His first stop was Jerry Bingham.

"Thanks, pal." Jerry grinned, grabbing the water and guzzling it down.

"Why are you always so nice to him?" the first bruiser complained.

"Hey, it's nice to be nice," Jerry said. "Besides" —he reached over and tousled Opera's hair— "rubbing this guy's head brings me good luck. Ain't that right, Opera?" He gave Opera a wink.

"Uh, yeah . . . ," Opera said. "Sure."

The two exchanged grins as Opera practically beamed over the attention . . . until

Bruiser Boy grabbed the other bottle from him and growled, "Yeah, well, luck or no luck, being nice to him or that . . ." He turned to Opera. "What's the name of that big-time loser friend of yours?"

"Which one?" Opera asked, "Wally or Wall Street?"

"Yeah, Wally McDorkoid—being nice to those morons gives us all a bad reputation." He rinsed out his mouth and spat the water onto the ground, making a nice little puddle of spit mud.

I wasn't too bugged hearing him make fun of me. After all, I worked long and hard for that reputation. But I was bothered when he gave Opera a push . . . so hard that my friend kinda stumbled and fell face-first into the fresh little puddle of spit mud. (I'd been giving Opera private coordination lessons for months, and it was almost encouraging to see them pay off. Almost.)

Of course, everyone busted a gut laughing. Everyone but me.

I was even more bugged when Opera tried to get up and Bruiser Boy stepped on his neck, pushing his face back down into the mud.

More laughter by them . . . more being bugged by me. In fact, I was so bugged that before I could stop myself I was racing out onto the field to try to help my friend. Now, normally

this was your typical McDoogle suicide mission.
You know the routine . . .

- ♣ Wally runs onto field to save friend.
- ♣ Wally makes total fool of himself.
- ♣ Wally gets turned into football shoe goo.

Yes sir, it was your standard, everyday affair.
However, this time, as you may recall, there was
something a little different about me.

Opera had barely gotten to his knees when
Bruiser Boy's foot came at him again. That's when
I sort of stepped in the way and sort of yelled,
"Why don't you pick on somebody your own size!"
(See what I mean about a suicide mission?)

The good news was, everyone was laughing
so hard, no one but Bruiser Boy heard me. The
bad news was, instead of landing on Opera's
neck, his big foot caught me in the gut and sent
me staggering halfway down the field. Unfortunately, this threw off his balance, causing him
to slip and

K-Splat!

join Opera in the spit mud.

Lots more laughter (this time at him) and
confusion (this time by him), as he looked

around trying to figure out what had happened. It was only then that I realized I might be able to take advantage of this invisible business. So, as Jerry helped Opera to his feet, and as my buddy hobbled off the field, I strolled quietly up to Bruiser Boy and waited for them to start playing again.

During practice, it was Bruiser's job to break through the line and tackle Jerry. But as luck would have it (along with some quick shoelace tying by yours truly), when the ball was snapped the big guy took one step forward and landed face-first on the ground—allowing Jerry to throw a perfect touchdown pass.

Lots of cheers and laughter.

The next play was even better. Everybody lined up, and, just before the ball was snapped, Bruiser Boy started giggling and swatting at his sides. (The fact that I was busy tickling him in the ribs might have had something to do with it.) It also had something to do with Jerry running past him for another touchdown.

On the next play a very baffled Bruiser Boy got to carry me piggyback a few yards before he finally stumbled and fell—allowing Jerry to throw another beautiful pass.

"What's going on?!" Bruiser shouted, leaping to his feet, looking all around. "What's happening?!"

By now everyone was rolling with laughter . . .
everyone but Coach Kilroy. "What's the matter
with you?!" he shouted at Bruiser from the side-
lines. "Tomorrow's the biggest game of the season. Either get yourself into this practice or hit
the showers!"

"Yes, Coach," Bruiser Boy said.

"Looks like you're having some bad luck,"
Jerry teased.

"I'll be all right," Bruiser Boy growled. He
got back on the line, once again preparing to
charge and tackle Jerry.

But before they started the next play, Jerry
called, "Hey, Opera, grab me a towel!"

Opera raced onto the field with a towel, and
once again Jerry gave his hair a tousle. "Sounds
to me like you just need some Opera luck," he
called to Bruiser.

By now the big guy was steaming. "I'll be
okay," he grumbled.

"Hey, Jer," his tall and gangly receiver said,
"let me have some of that luck."

"Help yourself." Jerry grinned.

Taking his cue, Opera lowered his head, letting
the receiver rub it.

"Me, too," Jerry's halfback said, trotting over
and giving Opera a rub.

Opera obliged.

"Thanks, pal." He slapped Opera on the shoulder, and Opera grinned back, obviously in waterboy heaven.

"Are you gonna play ball or what?" Bruiser yelled.

"Sure you don't want a shot?" Jerry teased, motioning to Opera.

"Let's play," Bruiser growled.

Jerry shrugged. "Just trying to help."

Opera ran off the field as they prepared for the next play. "Ready," Jerry called to his right. Then turning to his left he shouted, "Set!"

Everyone took his position on the line . . . including yours truly. I wasn't sure what to do next . . . though the string Bruiser Boy used to tie up his pants looked awfully inviting. I reached over to it but didn't have time to finish the job before Jerry yelled:

"Hike!"

The ball was snapped to Jerry, and he faded back to make another pass. Bruiser Boy broke past me and raced toward him. I watched in horror as the big guy headed straight for him. I had to do something. Somehow I had to stop him. With no other solution in mind, I raced for Bruiser as fast as I could and lunged at him, trying to tackle him.

But, of course, me tackling Bruiser Boy is

like a mosquito attacking a semitruck's wind-shield at sixty-five miles per hour. Still I man-aged to get my arms around the big guy's legs . . . until he slipped out. That was the bad news. The good news was, when he slipped out of my arms, he also slipped out of his pants!

That's right, they dropped to around his knees and

K-Oaafff!

Bruiser Boy fell face-first into, you guessed it, the spit mud . . . allowing Jerry to fire off another perfect touchdown pass.

After everyone was done laughing and slap-ping Jerry on the back (and after Coach had yanked Bruiser off the field and sent him to the showers), all the players started calling for Opera—so they could rub his head and have some of Jerry's luck for themselves.

It was a beautiful sight. And the rest of that afternoon I was more than a little busy—help-ing all those who had rubbed Opera's head to look great, and all those who wouldn't to look bad. In fact, in less than an hour I had turned my best friend around from being the team's joke . . . to being their prized mascot. It was a great feeling to help like that. Suddenly, being invisible wasn't so bad. In fact, it was pretty good.

Well, except for the two strangers in dark suits watching from the stands. The two strangers who constantly spoke into the microphones hidden in their coat sleeves. The two strangers who would very, very soon be turning the good times into bad ones.

Chapter 4

So Far, So Not-So-Good

I gotta tell you, except for not being able to

gurgle, gurgle, gurgle . . .

eat, I was really getting into this invisible kid stuff. Imagine doing anything you wanted without getting busted. And it didn't have to stop with helping Opera. Oh, sure, it was fun turning him into the team's good luck charm. But did it have to stop there? Couldn't I continue the team's "good luck" by "helping them out" during tomorrow's big game? And what about Wall Street's haunted house? Who knew how much fun that could be, let alone how much money we could make?

Of course, somewhere in the back of my brain I still knew it was a little like cheating (all right, it was *a lot* like cheating). But didn't

Wall Street have a point? Was cheating really that bad? I mean, as long as you didn't get caught?

"Hey, Wally . . . ," Wall Street whispered to me as we headed down the street on our way home. She motioned toward the Cineplex we were passing. "Check it out. *Attack of the Killer Bunny Slippers* is still playing."

"Cool," I said.

"Burp!" Opera agreed.

Now, don't let the title fool you. *Attack of the Killer Bunny Slippers* is the scariest horror film of all time. So bad that everyone in our school wanted to see it. But since it was rated R (as in g*R*uesome) it was definitely out of our league.

"Why don't you go in and check it out?" Wall Street asked.

"Me?" I croaked. "I'm not old enough. They'll stop me at the door."

"Not if they can't see you."

I turned to her. She was getting that grin on her face again . . . the one she had just before we turned on the OOPS, the one that made me more nervous than a turkey on Thanksgiving, a candy cane on Christmas, a chocolate bunny on—well, you get the picture.

I did my best to stall, using my famous and proven "Uhh . . ." routine.

"Go ahead, nobody will know."

"Uhh . . . uhh . . ."

"Maybe you'll get some ideas to use for our haunted house."

"Uhh . . . uhh . . . uhh . . ."

So much for my vocabulary skills. Fortunately, Opera came to my rescue. Good ol' Opera, a friend to the end, dependable, trustworthy:

"Yeah, Wally, *belch*, don't be such a chicken."

(See what I mean?)

My mind spun, my gears turned, my stomach

gurgle, gurgle, gurgled . . .

Then, in a sudden flash of inspiration (more like a dim spark of ignorance), I had my excuse. "I, uh, I don't have any money!"

They both cocked their heads and gave me a look that said, "Nice try, but do you really think our brain wattage is that low?"

"What?" I asked.

"You're invisible," Wall Street said. "You don't ever have to pay for anything again."

"Oh, yeah," I answered quietly.

And so, with the same enthusiasm as a kid heading off to summer school, I trudged toward the line of people waiting to enter the theater.

"Take good notes!" Wall Street called.

Gurgle, gurgle, gurgle . . .

my stomach replied.

"What's that sound?" the woman in front of me asked as she turned to her husband. "Is your acid indigestion acting up?"

"Not mine," he mumbled. "Thought it was you getting all gassy again."

For obvious reasons, I quickly moved past them and through the door.

So far, so good.

Next came the problem of finding a seat. Actually, finding a seat wasn't as bad as keeping it. Because, just as soon as I plopped down into an empty one, somebody would plop down on top of me.

"Oaff!" I'd groan.

"EEEK!" they'd scream.

After two or three times of practicing this delightful ritual, I figured it was better just to stand. If that's the worst of my problems, I had nothing to worry about.

Unfortunately, it wasn't, and I did . . .

Oh, sure, it was lots of fun going around sipping people's sodas without them knowing: "What's with these tightwads?" some guy complained. "They only give you half a cup now!"

Or eating their popcorn (it was too dark for anybody to see my stomach): "Keep your paws out of my popcorn!" some woman yelled at the stranger beside her.

But that was as good as it got. Because soon they started showing the movie. I don't want to gross you out, so I'll just tell you the parts that *weren't* incredibly gory and sickeningly gruesome.

Let's see, first there was:

Then there was:

And finally:

Hmm, I guess *all* the parts were incredibly gory and sickeningly gruesome—which would explain why, when I walked out of the theater, I was incredibly numb and sickeningly sick. Numb, sick, and constantly searching the sidewalk for any scurrying bunny slippers with an appetite for human flesh.

I felt awful. Worse than awful. And there was nothing I could do about it.

Not only was there the guilt from sneaking
into the theater, but also there were those awful
scenes from the movie. I tell you, if I could have
used a bucket of soap and a scrub brush to wash
them out of my mind, I would have. But there
was nothing I could do to get rid of them. They
wouldn't leave me on the way home, they wouldn't
leave me when I went upstairs to my room, and
they wouldn't leave when I tried to go to sleep that
night. Every time I closed my eyes, I saw dead
bodies and burping bunny slippers with blood-
stains around their cute little whiskers.

Finally, with no other solution, I reached for
Ol' Betsy and snapped her on. Maybe getting
back to my superhero story would help clear my
brain.

Then again, maybe . . .

When we last left SuperSlob, he'd
just been attacked by the notorious,
not-so-nice nut case...Neat Freak!

Already his room looks cleaner—
now you can actually catch glimpses
of his green carpeting (or is that
mold?)——and his dark brown walls (or
is that dried chocolate syrup?). And
then, just when things can't get any

neater, our hero feels his hair starting to untangle!

He turns to his mother in desperation. "Mom, what's happening? My hair
is combing itself!!"

"I don't know," she cries, trying
not to clap in delight. "But it looks
like you can kiss those dreadlocks
good-bye!"

And still things grow worse.
Suddenly

...*pppiiiRRR*

SuperSlob looks down and sees the
giant rip in his T-shirt repairing itself. Not only that, but his favorite
mustard stain (the cool one right up
front where everybody can see it) is
disappearing before his very eyes!

Is there no end to the tenacious
torture this tyrant is touting? (Looks
like it's time to hit the ol' dictionary. And while you're at it, flip over
to the *N*s....) Is there no way to nul-
lify his notorious neatness?

Nobody knows what made Neat Freak
so nutsoid about neatness. Some say

it happened when he was a baby. Rumor
has it that his family ran out of
windshield wiper fluid while driving
through Minnesota and he had to stare
through the bug-splattered windshield
for too many hours. Others say it came
from going to a museum and looking for
an entire day at all those messy
paintings they call modern art.

But whatever the cause, it was
enough to cause this crazed kid to
crack. Soon he was alphabetizing all
the little noodles in his alphabet
soup. Next, he was carefully arrang-
ing all those little grains of sand
(or whatever they are) in the family's cat box. And finally, worst of
all worsts, he flew to New York to
try to fill in the gap between David
Letterman's teeth.

"EXCUSE ME, MY DEAREST SON."
SuperSlob spins around to stare at
his mother as she continues to speak.

"I BELIEVE, IF IT IS NOT TOO
DIFFICULT, YOU SHOULD
PROCEED TO STOP NEAT
FREAK AT YOUR EARLIEST
POSSIBLE CONVENIENCE."

"Mom, what's wrong with your voice? You're talking all funny."

His mom's eyes widen in horror.

"I AM NOT CERTAIN, BUT SOME-HOW, AS I ATTEMPT TO SPEAK IN ONE MANNER, MY WORDS ARE CHANGED SO THAT MY SENTENCES SAY SOMETHING ENTIRELY DIFFERENT."

"Oh, no," our hero cries. "It's him! Neat Freak is even changing the way people speak!"

Without stopping to think of a plan (that would be far too orga-nized), SuperSlob races outside to save the day. But it's worse than he fears. Everyone is dressed in identi-cal clothes, navy blue suits for men, navy blue dresses for women. The cars are navy blue, too. Even the sky is, you guessed it, navy blue...well, except for the little white clouds that are spaced perfectly apart fill-ing the entire sky.

"Neat Freak!" our hero shouts to no one in particular. "Where are you? What's going on?!"

"I WAS GREATLY CONCERNED

THAT YOU WOULD NEVER ASK
THAT QUESTION."

Our hero's jaw drops open in sur-
prise. Everyone on the street has
turned to him. And they are *all*
speaking in unison. Everyone is saying exactly the same thing at the
same time:

"SUPERSLOB, I HAVE RELEASED
ONE GAZILLION AND SIX MICRO-
SCOPIC ROBOTS UPON THE PLAN-
ET. THEY ARE TAKING OVER THE
WORLD AND WILL SOON MAKE
EVERYTHING IN IT NEAT AND
TIDY."

SuperSlob watches in stunned
silence as people's jaws open and
close—while they look to each other
in fear, unable to stop their own
mouths from speaking.

"Is that how you're making all
these people dress the same and talk
alike?" he shouts. "With microscopic
robots??"

"THAT IS CORRECT. WITH
EVERYONE SPEAKING AND
PERFORMING IDENTICAL
MOVEMENTS, THE WORLD

IS BECOMING EVER SO
MUCH NEATER AND TIDIER."

"You can't do that!" our hero
shouts. "You can't have everything
the same. You can't expect
EVERYONE TO WEAR THE SAME
CLOTHES AND SAY THE SAME
THING AND DRIVE THE SAME—"

Suddenly, our hero grabs his mouth.
Great goober peas, the "perfect-
speak" is even happening to him! The
tiny robots are taking control of the
muscles in his own jaw. Is there no
way of being free from this fiendish
foe with the neurotic neatness? Does
this mean we'll always have to make
our beds, that we'll always have to
change our underwear? And don't even
get me started about the flossing.

These and other weighty questions
burn in our hero's mind, when suddenly—

"Hey, Wally, you in there?" It was my older
brother Burt (or was it Brock?).

I looked up from Ol' Betsy. "Yeah," I said, my
voice doing its usual cracking routine.

"Didn't see you at dinner."

"I, uh. . . ." Quickly I leaped under my covers. The last thing I needed was for him to see I was invisible. "I, uh, I wasn't hungry."

There was a moment's pause.

"Please, Lord," I prayed, "don't let him get all sensitive and open the door to check up on me."

Finally, he answered. "Well, just 'cause you ain't eatin' dinner don't mean you get off doin' the dishes."

Good ol' Brock (or was it Burt?). Thank You, God.

"I'll be down a little later," I called.

"Good. Oh, and a couple guys were here looking for you this afternoon."

"Guys?" I asked.

"Yeah, from the NBA or CIA or something like that."

"You don't remember which?" I asked.

"Nah, they all sound alike. But they wore fancy suits and kept on speaking into their sleeves like them Secret Service guys on TV. Kinda cool."

I frowned. "What did they want?"

"Didn't say, but I bet you'll find out."

My frown deepened. Unfortunately, he was right . . . righter than either of us would know. . . .

Chapter 5

"Anybody Got a Rolaid?"

The next morning I didn't know which was worse . . . being invisible, or having had a grand total of 23.8 seconds of sleep the night before. I don't want to say that sneaking into the movie affected me, but every time I closed my eyes I saw furry pink bunny slippers nibbling my toes, or making plans under my bed to take over the world, or breaking into Burt and Brock's room to gobble them up in one swift gulp. (Okay, maybe not every dream was bad, but you get the picture.)

No wonder I spent the next day practically sleepwalking through school . . . which would explain my stumbling into a kid in front of me, falling down, and causing a forty-seven-student pileup in the middle of the hallway . . . or clearing out the entire cafeteria when I fell asleep. (Actually, it wasn't the falling asleep that cleared everyone out, it was my head dropping onto one of the table's pepper shakers, causing me to have a sneezing attack.)

"ACHOO!"

"God bless you," Kid 1 at the table said.
"I didn't sneeze," Kid 2 at the table said.

"ACHOO! ACHOO!"

"Well, I didn't sneeze," Kid 1 at the table said.

"ACHOO! ACHOO! ACHOO!"

"Well, if you didn't sneeze and I didn't sneeze, then who—"

"ACHOO! ACHOO! ACHOO! ACHOO!"

Soon every eye in the cafeteria was turning to me . . . well, at least, to my vacant seat. And I don't suppose I helped matters much by suddenly reaching for a napkin and . . .

HOOOONKA!

blowing my nose.

"Augh! Augh!" Kid 1 screamed.

"A ghost! A ghost!" Kid 2 screamed.

To which I immediately leaped to my feet, crying, "Where?! Where?!"

To which everyone in the place pointed in the direction of my floating napkin and unexplained voice and screamed, "THERE! THERE!"

Later, of course, Wall Street tried to smooth things over by saying it was the ghost from the haunted house that had come to pay us a visit. And if they didn't believe her, they could swing by the place tonight right after the game. "Just a mere $7.95 admission (seniors and babies half price)."

Good ol' never-miss-a-buck Wall Street.

Unfortunately, that was about as good as things got. (You don't even want to hear about the kid trying to use the same stall as me in the boys' room.) Then there was fifth-period math class. . . .

"Wally," Opera whispered as we entered the room. "Where are you?"

"Right here," I whispered beside him.

"Listen, you gotta give me a hand."

"How's that?"

"Neil Anderthol, over there." He pointed to Bruiser Boy from yesterday's football practice. "He's been rubbing my head all day saying I

better give him luck to pass this math test or
there's going to be trouble."

"Trouble?" I asked.

"Yeah, like broken bones or the removal of
my vital organs."

"What can I do?" I asked.

"If you'd just sneak the answer sheet off
Miss Finklestein's desk and somehow let him
see it—"

"Opera!" I whispered. "That's cheating!"

"Yeah, I know, but this time it's for a good
cause—the SPCO."

I took a wild guess. "The Society for the
Prevention of Cruelty to Opera?"

"Bingo," he said, glancing over at Bruiser
Boy, who was giving him his best *this-better-
work-or-you're-dead-meat* sneer. "Please, Wally,
I really need your help, just this once."

"Opera . . ."

"If he doesn't pass the test, he'll get kicked
off the team and I'll get kicked halfway to
Neptune. Please, Wally, please . . ."

Now, look, I know what you're going to say—
cheating is wrong, and after sneaking into that
movie and after that little matter of getting
turned invisible by OOPS, shouldn't I have
learned my lesson? Well that, dear reader, I can
answer in one simple word—

"No, not yet!"
(All right, that was three simple words,
but I'm a writer, not a mathematician.)

So, even though I knew I shouldn't, once
Miss Finklestein called roll (for which I was
again absent), and once she passed out the test,
I went to work.

Actually, it was pretty easy. I just strolled up
to her desk, waited until she wasn't looking,
opened the folder, and pulled out the answer
sheet. Then it wasn't too hard to quietly lower it
to the floor out of everybody's sight and scoot it
toward Bruiser Boy's desk. After that, all I did
was tap him on the shoulder to get him to look
the other way while I quietly slipped it onto his
desk.

Now, it was just a matter of getting him to
turn back to his desk and

gurgle . . . gurgle . . . gurgle . . .

Uh-oh. My stomach was starting in again.
I'd been doing a pretty good job of fighting off
the hunger with plenty of water from the drink-
ing fountain and some clear chicken broth I
found in the cafeteria. Yum. Unfortunately, by
the sound of things, it wasn't quite . . .

gurgle . . . gurgle . . . gurgle

good enough.

Some of the nearby kids looked in our direction and snickered at the sound. Bruiser Boy
glanced around. Unfortunately, he still hadn't
seen the paper. My stomach grew

gurgle . . . gurgle . . . gurgle

louder. There was more laughter as more eyes
looked in our direction as I continued to

gurgle . . . gurgle . . . gurgle

even louder, causing them to laugh even harder,
causing Miss Finklestein to look up from her
desk. "Neil? Are you okay?"

"Yes, ma'am."

gurgle . . . gurgle . . . gurgle

"Are you *sure* you don't have to go to the rest
room?"

"Yes, ma'am." Unfortunately, it was about
this time that he finally glanced down and spotted the answer sheet on his desk . . .

causing his eyes to widen to the size of saucers . . .
causing my nervous stomach to really let loose . . .

gurgle . . . gurgle . . . gurgle

causing him to accidentally knock the paper to
the floor . . .
causing Miss Finklestein to rise to her feet . . .
causing him to unsuccessfully reach for the
paper with his foot . . .
causing Miss Finklestein to quickly approach . . .
causing him to try even harder with his foot . . .

gurgle . . . gurgle . . . gurgle

causing Miss Finklestein to arrive and pick up
the paper . . .
causing Bruiser Boy to mutter, "Oh, boy" . . .
causing Miss Finklestein to exclaim, "Why, Neil
Anderthol, I'm shocked" . . .
causing him to whine, "I don't know how it got
there" . . .
causing Miss Finklestein to escort him to the
principal's office . . .
finally, causing our star lineman on the football
team to be expelled from school and from being
able to play in tonight's big . . .

gurgle . . . gurgle . . . gurgle

game.

* * * * *

Ah, yes, the game . . .

When it finally rolled around the massacre wasn't as bad as I'd feared. It was nearly half-time, and we were only behind 54-0. But the good news was, nobody had gotten too hurt or needed too many organ transplants . . . yet. Though Jerry Bingham, that nice guy who's our quarterback, was sure getting hit

"Oaff!"

and tackled

"Oaff! Oaff!"

a lot

"Oaff! Oaff! Oaff!"

"Wally," Opera whispered to me from the side-lines, "you've got to do something. They're killing

Jerry. Without Neil Anderthol to block for him, he has no protection."

I looked out to the field. At the moment, five or six players were climbing off Jerry. At least I thought it was Jerry . . . it was hard to see over the rim of the big Jerry-shaped crater they'd just left in the field.

I knew it would be cheating again, but the guy definitely needed my help. Besides, wasn't I the one who'd gotten Bruiser Boy expelled in the first place?

So, reluctantly, I headed out onto the field.

"Ready," Jerry yelled. The team got into position. "Set . . . Hike!"

The ball was snapped to Jerry, and he headed back to make a pass. It would have been a good play except for the four body crushers breaking through the line and heading straight for him. He cocked his arm, trying to throw the ball, but it was obvious he wasn't going to make it. So, utilizing my mighty McDoogle mind (a scary process in the best of times), I leaped up, grabbed the ball out of his hand, and started running with it.

I knew it wasn't my brightest move . . . especially when the entire stadium gasped in astonishment (something about footballs floating across the field by themselves can look kinda odd). So, spotting the closest player to me, I figured I'd slip it into his hands. A good idea, except for the part in which he was so freaked out seeing the ball floating toward him that he screamed, turned, and ran for his life.

"Wait," I shouted, racing after him. "Take this with you, take this with you!"

By now everyone on both teams had stopped and was staring. Well, everyone but the guy I was trying to give the ball to. He just kept on running down the field screaming his head off, and I just kept on chasing after him shouting, "Take this with you, take this with you!"

But there was no reasoning with him. He just kept running and screaming and looking over his shoulder until he entered the end zone and

K-THUD!

slammed into the goal post head-first.

The big guy didn't fall right away. He sort of *stagger, stagger, staggered* to the left, then *stagger, stagger, staggered* to the right. This almost gave me enough time to catch up to him before he fell face-first into the mud . . . almost. But that didn't stop me. No sir, I didn't run all that way wheezing my lungs out for nothing. Instead of giving up, I brought the ball to a stop, hovered over him a second, then bent down and stuffed it into the back of his pants.

Everyone on the field watched in stunned silence. Come to think of it, so did everyone in the stands. Then finally, after a couple of lifetimes, one of the refs slowly raised his hands and halfheartedly tweeted his whistle. "Touchdown," he mumbled, shaking his head in disbelief, "I guess . . ."

The crowd cheered, and the band began to play.

Well, now, I thought, still gasping for breath and trying not to pass out, *that wasn't so hard.* I glanced at the scoreboard—54-6. *Only eight more touchdowns to go.*

A moment later, the halftime whistle blew, which meant the fun and games were over for a while. At least for the players.

Unfortunately, for me, they'd just begun. . . .

Chapter 6

Suit Guys Say, "Hi"

Down in the locker room at halftime Coach Kilroy was giving the football team their usual pep talk:

"I've never seen such a bunch of losers . . . no, make that such a bunch of untalented losers . . . no, make that such a bunch of lazy, untalented losers . . . no, make that such a bunch of—"

Well, you get the picture. Apparently, he never quite grasped the difference between *dis*couragement and *en*couragement. (Hey, one prefix is as good as another, right?) So, now everybody sat on the bench breaking into uncontrollable sobs, having nervous breakdowns, or calling for their mommies, when suddenly:

gurgle . . . gurgle . . . gurgle

Coach came to a stop. "What was that?" he asked.

Call me overcautious, but given my last run-in with this sound, I immediately sprinted toward the bathroom and locked myself in a stall where nobody could hear me. Halftime wouldn't last forever. And when it was over, I'd get back out onto the field and make another couple hundred touchdowns.

Until then, with plenty of time to kill, I grabbed a nearby roll of toilet paper, pulled out a pen, and went back to work on my superhero story.

When we last left SuperSlob, he was out on the streets looking for the frantically fiendish and foolishly fraudulent . . .

(more scary music, please . . .)

Neat Freak! More important, he was looking for a way to stop Freak's millions of microscopic robots from tidying up the world so we won't have to wash out the tub when we're done taking baths and can leave our shirttails untucked.

In a flash of super inspiration (along with the incredible imagination of a very close writer friend of his) SuperSlob reaches to his

Superhero wrist band (just $19.95 at
Superheroes-R-Us stores everywhere) and
presses the button marked:

"PRESS THIS BUTTON
TO FIND BAD GUY'S
ROBOTS"

Immediately, a magnifying glass flips down
from his Superhero baseball cap (sold at those
same Superheroes stores), allowing him to see one
of the pesky little machines crawling up his arm.
Not only can he see it, he can actually hear it.

"Danger, Danger," it shouts. "Warning,
Warning!"

"Hey," SuperSlob calls.

"Danger, Warning, Warning, Danger."

"Aren't you the robot from that old <u>Tossed
in Space</u> TV series?

Immediately the little robot stops. "Why, yes,
I am." He clears his throat hopefully. "Are you a
fan?"

"Weren't you a lot bigger in the series?"

"I was sick awhile back and lost some
weight." Then, continuing, he adds, "Would you
like an autographed picture? I have some in
the trunk of my car."

"Uh, maybe later," SuperSlob says. "But

tell me, what are you doing in my story?"

"There's not much call for TV robots these days, so I work where I can."

"But you're working for a bad guy."

"Yeah, but he's got good medical benefits, and I get two weeks' paid vacation."

"Yeah, but—"

"Look, I'd love to talk, but coffee break isn't for another hour, so if you'll excuse me, Warning, Warning! Danger, Danger!"

Suddenly he fires his laser arm at one of SuperSlob's freckles.

Zap!

"Ow! What are you doing?!"

"Just rearranging some of these freckles so we have a nice straight—

Zap!

"Ow!"

—line."

"You can't do that!" SuperSlob cries.

"I can do whatever I want. This is the goofy superhero story, remember?"

"I know, but—"

Zap!

"Ow!"

*And then, suddenly, before there are any
more rearranged freckles—*

The door to my stall flew open, and there stood
two FBI guys. The same two fellows who had been
watching us from the stands the day before. And
how could I tell they were FBI? It wasn't easy, but
there was something about the way they both
stood with their guns aimed at me . . . then, of
course, there were their dark blue Windbreakers
with the giant letters "FBI" printed on them.
Other than that it was just a lucky guess.

"Freeze!" they both shouted.

No problem, I was already frozen . . . in ter-
ror.

"Put down that toilet paper and come out
with your hands up!" the head guy ordered.

I obeyed and set down the toilet paper roll I
was writing my story on.

"Slowly . . . ," he said, pointing his gun in the
direction he thought I should be, "slowly . . ."

"L-l-l-ook," I squeaked, "if this is about helping Neil Anderthol cheat . . ."

"Be quiet and keep those hands up."

Of course, he couldn't see if my hands were up or not, but that didn't stop me from obeying. As I stepped out, I saw Opera, standing nearby with another agent as well as the lady scientist who had taken us on the tour of the OOPS laboratory.

"Wally," Opera called in my direction. "They know what happened."

"They do?" I croaked.

"That's right," the head guy said, "and we want to help you." Then turning to the science lady, he added, "Isn't that right, Ms. Simpson?"

She gave a nervous twitch that looked like it was supposed to be a smile.

"I said, 'Isn't that right, Ms. Simpson?'"

She glanced around nervously and finally croaked out a feeble, "Yes."

Head Guy turned back to me. "There, you see, everybody is on your side. We all want to help."

But that was all Science Lady could take. Suddenly she shouted, "No! It's not true!"

Head Guy turned back to her and shouted, "We had a deal!"

"He's just a boy!"

"Simpson, we had a—"

But she kept right on talking, squeezing in as many words as possible before they could stop her. "They want to use you as a secret agent, Wally! Don't listen to them! They want to—"

"Shut her up!" Head Guy shouted to the third agent.

"They want you to sneak around the country and do all sorts of—"

"Get her out of here! Take her and Tub-O, there, and get them out of here!"

Third Agent Guy grabbed her and Opera's arms and half-dragged, half-pushed them toward the door. But not before Science Lady managed to shout:

"Don't listen to them, Wally! Meet me at the lab. I'll be there tonight! I can help you! I can—"

That was all she said before they slammed the door shut behind her.

I glanced around. Coach Kilroy and the team had already headed back out onto the field. It was just me and my two new agent pals.

"Now get on the floor with your arms spread," Head Guy barked.

I nodded. "Yes, sir." My hands shook so hard that when I tried to put my pen into my pocket I accidentally dropped it on the floor. I'd had it on me when I turned invisible, so it had turned invisible, too. But it made quite a racket. I quickly bent down to scoop it up, repeating, "Yes, sir."

"That's a good boy," he said, looking down to where the noise and my voice had been.

But I wasn't there anymore. I'd straightened up to put the pen in my pocket, yet he still thought I was on the floor.

"Now then . . . ," he said, grabbing a pair of handcuffs on his belt and kneeling to the floor. "Ms. Simpson was just a little hysterical, that's all. No one's going to hurt you, son. In fact, I bet you'll have the time of your life working for us."

He reached out, trying to find my arm.

It was only then that I realized—if I were quiet, I could step around him. And if I could step around him, I could sneak past him. And if I could sneak past him, I could get out of the room. Ever so quietly, I inched my way around him as he kept right on talking.

"You've seen those James Bond movies, right?" He continued reaching for where he thought my arm was. "Wouldn't it be just swell to get to be a spy like that?" Still more reaching on his part.

Still more inching past him on mine.

"Well, you can be that and more."

By now, I was halfway to the door.

"Drive around in those fancy cars."

More reaching.

More inching.

"Play with all those neato keen gadgets."
I arrived at the door. Slowly, I opened it.
"Get to beat up all those bad guys."
Carefully, I slipped through it.
"Oh, sure, there may be some dangers, but—"
And, ever so quietly, started to close it when

gurgle . . . gurgle . . . gurgle

Both agents spun around to the door.

gurgle . . . gurgle . . . gurgle

"After him!!"
I would have loved to stick around and chat,
maybe exchange addresses, ask to see the latest
pictures of the kids. But at the moment I had a
few other things on my mind, like, oh, I don't
know . . .

RUNNING FOR MY LIFE!!

Chapter 7

Let the Chase Begin

I raced out of that building faster than Dad disappears on Saturday mornings to play golf. Part of me wanted to stick around and keep helping the football team, but another part of me wanted to live. Call me selfish, but for some reason the wanting to live part won out. Go figure . . .

But what about Wall Street?

They'd already captured Opera. I had to warn her before it was too late. Of course, there was the usual, "Stop, stop, we'll shoot, we'll shoot!" coming from my FBI pals as they raced out of the locker room after me. But since they couldn't exactly see whom they were stop, stopping, much less shoot, shooting, I figured I was okay.

I ran to the football field and quickly checked out the bleachers. Wall Street was nowhere to be seen. She must have already left to start making

those big bucks at the haunted house. I twirled
around and took off after her.

By the time I arrived at the house, I was
gasping for air. (Hey, a half block can really
wear a guy out . . . especially a guy in my great
shape.) A line of ten or fifteen people had
already formed on the steps leading up to the
porch.

"Yes sir, ladies and gentlemen," Wall Street
called from a table in front of the door, "just
$12.95 and you can witness all the ghouls, gob-
lins, and ghosts in action."

"I thought you said $7.95," some guy com-
plained.

"I know," Wall Street said, shaking her head.
"Isn't inflation terrible?"

I raced toward the steps wheezing my lungs
out. "Wall Street, Wall Street!"

Hearing my voice, the people in line jumped
back. "What's that?" they shouted.

Wall Street frowned. "Sounds like our ghost
friend has been doing a little jogging."

"Wall Street," I shouted, stumbling up the
steps, "you gotta listen to me!"

She tilted back her head, closed her eyes,
and answered, "Yes, O great spirit, I hear your
attempts to communicate from beyond. Tell us,
tell us what message do you wish to—"

But that's all she got out before I arrived . . . well, if you call tripping over the last step, crashing into her money table, and sending it, the money, and myself sprawling onto the porch "arriving."

"AUGH!" the people screamed in fright.

"Not to worry," Wall Street cried. "It's just his little way of saying hi."

"Well, I gots a way of makin' him say goodbye," a voice cackled from the back of the line.

I looked up to see a crazy old man with crazy white hair sticking out from under a yellow construction worker's hat. He was approaching the porch. He had a gizmo attached to his back (which looked a lot like a fire extinguisher), and he held a black nozzle attached to the gizmo (which looked a lot like a fire extinguisher hose). On top of his hard hat were two little radar dishes that rotated back and forth and kept on

beep, beep, beeping.

"Who are you?" Wall Street asked.

"Iggy Norant, Spirit Exterminator, at your service." He shoved a business card at her. "If ghosts ain't yer cup o' tea, I'm the one to make 'em flee."

Wall Street glanced around nervously. "Well, actually, this ghost is kind of a good—"

Unfortunately, that was about the time I rose to my feet. Which would have been okay, if I hadn't risen into him, which sent him staggering backward.

"Augh!" Iggy screamed. "He's on the attack, he's on the attack!" With these words ringing in everyone's ears, he reached to his backpack gizmo, flipped a switch, and suddenly a greenish liquid began to

HIISSSSS . . .

out of his hose, spraying in all directions.

Of course, everybody panicked, doing their usual shouting, screaming, and fainting routine. And, of course, Iggy tried his best to calm them down with such reassuring words as: "Don't worry, folks, I'm a professional. He'll only be able to kill a few of you before I get him!"

"What is that stuff?" Wall Street cried, trying to dodge the green liquid as it sprayed in her direction.

"Gatorade," Iggy yelled back. "Gets 'em every time."

And get me, it did. Before I could duck for cover, ol' Iggy managed to cover me in the sticky green liquid. Now, normally you'd think this wouldn't be a problem since I was invisible . . . except (and there's always an except in these stories) the part of me that got wet could now be seen as a shiny, green outline.

"Augh!" the people screamed. "The ghost is appearing to us! The ghost is appearing to us!"

To which Wall Street, always the quick thinker, added, "That'll be an extra two dollars! That'll be an extra two dollars!"

Seeing my outline, Iggy turned his hose on full force. "Take that, you foul varmint from Hades!"

Now, everybody saw me—or at least the green liquid that was sticking to me. Having no clue what to do, but getting tired of drowning in Gatorade, I turned and ran into the house . . . which would have been okay, except that I was followed by the shouting Iggy, "You can run, but you can't hide!" . . . who was followed by the screaming mob, "Get him good! Get him good!" . . . who was followed by the yelling Wall Street, "Better make that three dollars! Better make that three dollars!"

I'll save you all of the gasping and wheezing details. Let's just say that after running a few hundred miles inside the house (with Iggy and the gang right behind me), I thought I'd try

some new scenery and check out what the base-
ment had to offer. Unfortunately, this would
involve the tiny detail of opening the door and
trying to run down the steps without falling,
which, of course, for me is a complete impossi-
bility. So, instead of running I sort of

bounce, bounce, bounced,
tumble, tumble, tumbled

down them until I hit the

"Oaff!"

concrete floor. But even that wasn't good
enough for a full-time klutz like me. I chose to
keep right on

roll, roll, rolling

across the floor until I hit the coal pile next to
the old-fashioned coal furnace. Actually, it
wasn't as much a coal pile as it was a pile of
coal dust, which would explain my

cough, cough, coughing.

It would also explain the new black outline

of coal dust that completely covered me as I rose to my feet.

"There he is!" Mob Member 1 shouted.

"We got him cornered!" Mob Member 2 cried.

"Stand back, folks," Iggy warned, "this is where it gets tricky." Slowly, he started toward me. "Nice ghosty, ghosty, ghosty." Doing his imitation of a smile, he held out his hand. "Come on, fella, nobody's gonna hurt you."

Call me suspicious, but somehow I had my doubts about not getting hurt. I glanced around. There was no way out. Well, except for the coal chute. The coal chute that I spun around to, and immediately scampered up!

"AFTER HIM!"

It took a little doing, but after a lot of slipping and sliding, I finally made it to the top of the chute. Now there was only the coal chute door, which I had to

BAMB, BAMB, BAMB,

a few million times before it finally gave way and opened. I stumbled out into the cold night air and my freedom.

Cold night air, yes. Freedom, well, not exactly . . .

"AFTER HIM!"

I spun toward the new voices. It was my FBI buddies. They'd just climbed out of their car and were racing at me.

"AFTER HIM!"

I turned back to the house. Iggy and my other pals were piling out of the front door and also coming at me.

Oh, boy! What fun.

Now don't get me wrong, I like parties as much as the next guy—especially when I'm the guest of honor. It's just when they start passing out FBI guns as party favors, and ghostbusting Gatorade for refreshment that I get a little nervous. Then there was that screaming mob. I'm sure they loved me dearly, but they didn't exactly look like they were going to break into a rousing chorus of "For He's a Jolly Good Fellow."

So, with no other alternative, I decided to do what I do best . . .

Run.

Run and

"AUGHHHHHhhhh . . ."

scream.

The only problem was, I had no idea where I should be running and screaming to. China was out of the question. And, though I hear

Antarctica is lovely this time of year, I left my decisions. Finally, I made up my mind and took off.

The good news was, the lab was not that far away and I knew a shortcut through our neighbors, the Lynches', backyard. The bad news was, the Lynches just got a brand-new dog. I'm not exactly sure what breed Muttly was—some sort of cross between a grizzly bear and a *Tyrannosaurus rex*—but I do know the type of teeth it had . . .

Sharp.

Yes sir, just as soon as I threw my feet over the fence and nimbly landed on the other side,

"OAFF!"

while breaking a minimal amount of body parts, I

GRRRRR . . .

"Nice doggie, doggie . . ."

CHOMP

"YEOW!"

knew what type of teeth it had.

Leaping to my feet, I dashed across the yard
as fast as I could (which isn't all that fast when
you have a *grizzly-saurus* attached to your
rear). Unfortunately, it was that new attach-
ment that sort of threw off my balance, causing
us both to

"AUGH . . ."
K-Splash

into the swimming pool.

After the usual thrashing, screaming for
help, and nearly drowning, I made it to the edge
of the pool and pulled myself out. The bad news
was, my little dip left a nasty Gatorade and coal-
dust ring around the pool. The good news was,
it washed me clean, allowing me to become
totally invisible again.

Yes sir, it was just like old times . . . which
allowed me to race to the fence without Muttly
practicing his *sink-teeth-into-Wally's-rear* routine.
It also allowed me to sneak up behind the critter
and (WARNING: IF YOU'RE AN ANIMAL
LOVER DO NOT READ THESE NEXT SIX
WORDS) tweak him soundly behind the ears.

(Hey, I warned you.)

The creature dashed off, howling and yelp-
ing, though it was difficult to hear him over my

own gruntings and groanings as I dragged my
body up and over the fence. Then, of course,
there was that nasty shattering sound that
bones make when you fall off high objects (like,
oh, say, high fences), drop through some lovely
branches, and hit something hard (like, oh, say,
a hard sidewalk).

Unfortunately, despite my long shortcut, I
hadn't lost my pursuers.

"There he is!" Iggy shouted as he rounded
the corner. "I see the branches moving."

I looked up and saw the old guy leading the
pack as they ran straight toward me. I leaped to
my feet. After resetting a broken leg or two, I
spotted one of those new scooter thingies in the
Lynches' front yard. And, never being shy to borrow toys from friends (just as long as I return
them in as few pieces as possible), I grabbed the
scooter, stumbled to the sidewalk, and took off.

For the most part it was a pleasant ride . . .
well, except for those barricades surrounding
that open manhole. Well, actually, the barricades that

"AUGH!"
K-RASH! K-RASH! K-RASH!

had been surrounding the open manhole.

But crashing through them wasn't nearly as annoying as

"AUGH!"
K-SPLASH

falling *into* the open manhole.

Still, such obstacles are a minor inconvenience when you're busy racing for your life. It's the other nuisances—like climbing out of the manhole, draining all that water from your lungs, and taking off on your scooter again . . . right through a major intersection—that get to be bothersome.

Actually, going through the intersection wasn't that big of a problem. It was that pesky traffic light that turned red just as I approached it. The one I would have stopped at if I knew where the brakes were. The one I breezed through at just slightly under the speed of sound. And even that wouldn't have been so bad if it weren't for those four cars coming from different directions. The ones that had to hit their brakes and swerve hard to miss me. Fortunately, they did miss me. Unfortunately, they didn't miss

SQUEAL
K-RASH

tinkle . . . tinkle . . . tinkle

each other.

Finally, there was that police car, which happened to have policemen in it, who happened to have seen the whole thing. For some reason they thought it would be a good idea to kick on their siren and flashing lights to join in the chase.

Yes sir, I was drawing quite a crowd. With Iggy, the mob, the FBI, a few angry drivers (with a few destroyed cars), and one very loud police car (complete with two policemen), it was getting to be quite a party.

Unfortunately, every party needs some games to break the ice. And, as I approached the lab, I couldn't help thinking that those games were about to begin. Come to think of it, the breaking was about to begin, too. But, as we all know, it wouldn't be the ice that was breaking. . . .

Chapter 8

Back to OOPS

The good news was, Science Lady had left the front doors unlocked and was waiting for me in the lobby. The bad news was, the TV crew for the news show *59½ Minutes* was also there.

I burst through the doors just as reporter Dan Rathernot was asking, "So tell us, Ms. Simpson, is there any truth to the rumor about your creating an invisible boy who runs around terrifying the citizens of this town?"

I don't know how he knew, but I appreciated Science Lady trying to sidestep the question. "Well, actually," she said, "that is, er, it all depends upon how you, uh, define the word, um, 'invisible.'"

She might have been able to stall a bit longer if I hadn't accidentally plowed into the cameraman . . .

"AUGH!"
K-Bang!
broken camera piece here
broken camera piece there
and another one right over there . . .

as well as the soundman

"LOOK OUT!"
K-Blamb!
broken microphone here
broken recorder there
and broken soundman right
over there . . .

"Wally, you're here!" Science Lady cried. Obviously it was a lucky guess on her part (either that or she'd read one of my books and knew all about my entrances).

Either way, I calmly rose to my feet and as gently as possible screamed my head off. "WHAT DO I DO? HOW DO I GET UN-INVISIBLE?!"

"Just follow me," she said as she ran to the lobby doors. She locked them and leaped back over the unconscious TV crew on her way to the next room.

I did my best to follow . . . though my leaping was a bit . . .

> *K-Bang!*
> *K-Blam!*

lame . . . which would explain why the TV crew,
who was just waking up, once again hit the floor
and returned to unconsciousville.

I did my best to untangle myself from all
their cords and cables as Science Lady stood at
the door crying, "Hurry, Wally! In here, hurry!"

At last I freed myself and headed toward
her. Meanwhile, a few well-meaning folks began
banging on the door. Folks like (and if you can
sing this to the tune of "The Twelve Days of
Christmas," good luck):

> *Five mob mem-bers . . .*
> *Four angry drivers,*
> *Three FBI,*
> *Two po-lice-men,*
> *And a friend trying to make an extra buck.*
> (Hey, you're good. Very good.)

At last, Science Lady slammed the door shut.

"OW!"

Then opening it, she tried again—this time
waiting until I was inside.

"You said you could help me," I cried. "You said you could make me un-invisible!"

"I can," she said, "but it will take time."

And then, right on cue

K-SLAM
tinkle-tinkle-tinkle . . .

my "Twelve Days of Christmas" pals finally crashed the party. (Well, at least the outside lobby doors.)

Science Lady locked the next set of doors. Then she reached out her hand to me, and we started running through the building toward the lab . . . locking each set of doors behind us as we went.

As we ran, she explained, "I reviewed the history of the OOPS computer program. I know what you did," she said. "And the only way to reverse the effects is for the beam to strike you again."

"Sounds easy enough," I wheezed as we ran.

"Except we'll have to reverse all of the programs to get to yours."

"Meaning . . ."

"Meaning we experimented with several objects before you used it. We'll have to go through each of those objects first."

"Meaning . . ."

"Meaning, it's going to take some time."

"Why can't you just cut to my program?"

"There are no shortcuts. You can't cheat with the OOPS. If you do, the whole system will malfunction."

There was that word again . . . *cheat*. It seemed every time I turned around someone was doing it. Unfortunately, that someone was usually me. Well, I'd learned my lesson. This time I'd do it the right way. Whatever it took, whatever she wanted, I'd do it. No cheating, no shortcuts. At least that's what I told myself as we entered the OOPS room.

Unfortunately, it didn't take long for me to change my mind. And unfortunatelier, with that changed mind came some even BIGGER changes. . . .

Chapter 9

Pick a Shape, Any Shape

Moments later, we entered the room, and there was the OOPS sitting just like it had the day my little nightmare began.

"Now," Science Lady said, "hop up on that seat over there, and I'll readjust the beam to strike you."

If you're thinking I was nervous or scared or anything like that, you're way wrong. I wasn't nervous or scared or anything like that . . .

I WAS PETRIFIED.

"A-a-are you sure th-th-th-is is the only way?" I stuttered.

"I'm afraid so." She flipped on the main power supply, and OOPS hummed to life. "I'll enter the past programs, beginning with our first experiment, and go through the list until we finally reach yours. When that happens, I'll activate the beam. It'll hit you for a split second, and the old Wally, the visible one, should return as good as new."

"Except for the dog bites, broken bones, and internal injuries," I said.

"Pardon me?"

"Never mind, it's a long story."

Although I was still nervous, I climbed up into the OOPS seat. Something about the approaching sounds of yelling, shouting, and breaking doors made me think we should probably hurry.

Science Lady took a seat beside me. In front of her was the computer keyboard. She cleared her throat. "Now, going through each program is going to take some time, so you'll have to be patient."

The shouting and door breakings grew closer. I glanced nervously at her keyboard. "Why can't you just hit that *SELECT ALL* key," I asked, "so we can get it all done at once?"

She pushed up her glasses. "As I said before, you can't cheat with the OOPS. We have to follow the correct procedure."

I gave a reluctant nod.

Outside, the shouting grew even louder. And then, just to liven things up, there were a few

BLAM! BLAM! BLAM!

gunshots.

I swallowed nervously.

So did Science Lady.

"Stand by," she said. She flipped a few more switches, and the OOPS hummed even louder. Almost loud enough to drown out the shouting and door poundings. *Almost.*

"They're just about here!" I yelled.

"Hang on," she said, doing her best to concentrate as the

BREAK, BREAK, BREAKing

of doors increased from outside, and the

drip, drip, dripping

of sweat increased from me.

Suddenly, there was a tremendous

BOOM!

that shook the entire room.

"They're at the lab door!" I shouted.

She glanced up. "It's made of steel. It will take them awhile to break through. But just to be safe . . ." She leaped from her stool and ran over to double-check the locks as the door continued to shake.

BOOM! BOOM! BOOM!

and the crowd continued to yell,

"THIS IS THE POLICE!"
"THIS IS THE FBI!"
"ANYBODY FOR MORE GATORADE?"

I glanced over to the computer keyboard . . .
particularly to the *SELECT ALL* key as the

BOOM! BOOM! BOOMings

continued. The door was starting to cave in. I
knew what Science Lady had said about cheating, and that we had to go through each of
OOPS's programs, but I also knew the door
wouldn't hold much longer. So, against my better
judgment, I reached for the *SELECT ALL* key.

BOOM! BOOM! BOOM!
"OPEN UP! OPEN UP!"
"I'LL HAVE TO CHARGE EVERYONE AN
EXTRA 75 CENTS FOR ADMISSION!"

Just then, Science Lady looked back to me.
She saw what I was doing. "No, Wally, don't!"
I hesitated, my finger hovering over the key

as the door continued to shake under the poundings, as the angry mob continued to yell.

Then, closing my eyes, I lowered my finger
and . . .

"NO, WALLY, DON'T!"

. . . hit it.

Of course, there were the usual

ZAAAP, K-RACKLE,
and *ZIIIPs*

with more than the usual amount of

FLASHes

and

"AUGHHHHHs!"

as the beam finally struck me. Yes sir, lots and
lots of

"AUGHHHHHs!"

"WALLY!" Science Lady cried. "WALLY, CAN
YOU HEAR ME?!" And then, suddenly . . .

It was over.

Just like that. The beam quit hitting me,

and all the special effects stopped doing their special effects things.

I opened my eyes and looked around. "Well, now, that wasn't too bad," I said, calmly glancing over to Science Lady.

But she was not calmly glancing back at me. Instead, she was staring in wide-eyed horror.

"What's wrong?" I asked.

Now it was her turn to stutter. "O-o-orange," she said, pointing a trembling finger at me.

"What?"

"O-o-range."

The best I figured, she meant my clothes had somehow turned orange . . . until I looked down at my body . . . at least at what used to be my body. Because instead of turning my clothes orange . . . it had turned me orange. But not the color, the fruit! That's right, suddenly I had become as round as, well, as an orange. Then, of course, there was the thick, dimply skin, and let's not forget the ever-popular navel right in my center.

"AHHH!" I screamed. "What happened!? What happened?"

"An orange was our very first experiment," she cried. "I told you not to hit the *SELECT ALL* key!"

"Yeah, but—" I stopped, surprised that I was

speaking through my navel. (I would have spoken through my mouth, but since oranges don't have mouths, not to mention arms, legs, or hands, I worked with what I had.)

"Now your body is going to morph into each of our past experiments until it finally reaches the last one, which will be you."

"No way!" I cried.

"I told you there were no shortcuts!" she shouted. "I told you there's no cheating with the—"

But that was as far as she got before the steel door finally exploded open. Yes sir, it was just like old times, with all my pals . . . the FBI, the angry mob, Iggy the Exterminator, the owners of four demolished cars, the police, the *59½ Minutes* TV crew, and, of course, my best buddy "Has-everybody-paid-their-extra-admission-fee?" Wall Street.

Unsure what to do, I leaped off the seat (actually rolled off since I no longer had leap-ers to leap with) and hit the floor.

"Wally!" Science Lady cried. But it was no use. I don't care how much she begged, I wasn't in the mood to become fresh-squeezed juice for the group. So I ran (er, make that *rolled*) toward the nearest door for my getaway.

"Is that him?" Iggy shouted. "Disguised as an orange?"

To which Science Lady, being the world's second-worst liar (check out *My Life As Dinosaur Dental Floss* for the worst), cried out, "What orange?! I don't see any orange!"

The crowd saw through her story, and apparently in need of their daily dose of vitamin C, took off toward me. "AFTER HIM!"

Needless to say, I continued to

roll . . . roll . . . roll.

Well, that's what I wanted to continue doing. But I felt a surge of energy shoot through my body, and suddenly I could no longer roll. You see, it's a little hard to roll when you've just become a giant, rectangular pink eraser. That's right. Just as it had taken awhile for my body to turn invisible when it was first hit with the OOPS, it was now taking awhile to go through each of the programs from the machine's past experiments. And, as best I could tell, experiment number two involved, you guessed it . . . a Pink Pearl eraser!

Of course, everyone did the usual gasp-and-faint routine . . . especially me. But eventually we all got bored with that, regained consciousness, and continued the chase.

"After him!" they shouted.

"   ," I replied. And for good reason.
You ever hear an eraser talk? This time I didn't
even have a navel to use.

And so the race continued . . . my pursuers
shouting and screaming while I tried to run
(with little success) then roll (with even less
success). I was getting nowhere fast, until I
finally realized that even though erasers can't
run, and we really can't roll, we sure can

bounce, bounce, bounce.

(So I quickly bounced toward the next door,
fighting the urge to rub out any penciled docu-
ments I passed along the way and doing my
best not to leave those ugly little eraser filings
behind me.) I looked over my shoulder, which
was a little tough since I no longer had a shoulder to look over—come to think of it, I no longer
had eyes to look with, either, which explains my
newly acquired habit of

K-Bamb—bounce, bounce, bouncing
K-Slam—bounce, bounce, bouncing

into every wall and desk in the room.

The good news was, this only lasted a moment.

The bad news was, well, that it only lasted a moment. I didn't know how many experiments they'd done with OOPS, but it looked like I was about to become number three. Once again I felt a strange electrical sensation rush through my body, and once again I changed.

This time I had legs and arms and hands and everything.

"All right!" I shouted (which meant I also had a mouth).

Things were getting better by the second . . . or so I thought. But the excitement was short-lived. Because I also noticed that I had a long, thick tail, that my arms and hands were purple, and that I had this overwhelming desire to start singing, "I love you, you love me . . ."

What was going on?!

It was only then that I caught a reflection of myself in one of the windows. Oh, great! Now I was some kid's stuffed animal. That's right, experiment number three involved a giant, purple, singing . . . dinosaur!

But before I could start dancing, much less give the crowd a lecture on how boys and girls should try to be nicer to each other, I felt that all-too-familiar electrical sensation. (Kinda like when I was stupid enough to stick my tongue on a battery—only instead of my tongue, it's my entire body, and instead of a battery, it's the giant electrical transformer at Grand Coulee Dam!) I knew it was time for another change, and I managed to race into the next room (a giant library, with lots of bookcases) before it happened.

Then, suddenly, my legs were gone, so was my color—along with that snappy little song. I could no longer see. I could no longer move. No rolling, no bouncing, no running. I was completely stationary, which would explain why the entire group of folks

BAMB . . . BAMB . . . BAMB . . .

slammed into me. Which almost, but not quite, explained the cracking sensation I felt running up and down my body. It wasn't until someone shouted, "A glass of water! He's turned into a glass of water!!" that I finally caught on.

Then someone else added, "And he's cracking!"

Now I understood, completely. I'd become a glass of water. And after all that slamming and bambing I was cracking.

"Look out!" Iggy screamed. "He's going to burst!"

And

K-WOASHHH

burst I did . . . all over the floor. I swept toward
them like a giant tidal wave.

"AUGH!" they screamed as some were
knocked down. The rest tried to keep their foot-
ing on the slippery floor. They tried, but

slip . . . "WHOA!"—*K-rash*
slip . . . "WHOA!"—*K-splat*
slip . . . "WHOA!"—*K-fall*

they didn't.

Yes sir, we were having great fun (and giving
the floor a good mopping while we were at it).
But all good things must come to an end. Soon,
I felt another one of those pesky tingling sensa-
tions. Sooner still, my water was sucked up, and
I could see again. In fact, I could see perfectly . . .
every detail of my pursuers, down to the tiniest
hairs on their heads (not to mention in their
noses). The reason was simple . . .

I'd turned into somebody's eyeglasses!

"Hang in there, Wally!" Science Lady
shouted from the back of the crowd. "Just two
more to go! Just two more programs before you
become Wally again!"

Great. I don't want to complain, but I was
starting to get an identity complex. I mean, I

didn't know if I was coming or going (let alone who I was coming and going as).

Speaking of going, as I glanced around the library, I spotted a door with an EXIT sign over it. If I could somehow get to it, if whatever I was about to become allowed me to move, then I still had a chance of getting away and—

There was that electrical sensation again. I waited breathlessly (not that eyeglasses have much breath to wait with) when suddenly I felt very thick and sluggish and . . . gooey. Very, very gooey.

"He's turned into a giant chocolate bar!" someone yelled.

"And he's melting! Fast!"

"Look out, he's oozing this way!"

And ooze I did. I'd gotten pretty hot and sweaty from all the running. And now the heat was melting me all over the floor. And apparently all over my pursuers.

"Eewww!" Head FBI Guy cried.

"Ee's got me feet!" Iggy screamed.

"I can barely move in this goop!" a police officer shouted.

They weren't the only ones. As best as I could tell, my thick chocolate-ness was clinging

to everyone. Talk about being spread too thin.
Talk about being in a sticky situation. Talk
about—well, that was enough talking. Now it
was just a matter of waiting for the final
transformation—waiting for me to become
Wally McDoogle again (and hoping they
wouldn't get the munchies and start nibbling
on me before I did).

"Please, God," I prayed, "bring me back to
normal. Please get me out of this mess. I've
learned my lesson. No more shortcuts, no more
cheating. Just help me get back to—"

The tingly sensation began again. But instead of becoming myself, I became a penny
(you thought I forgot that one, didn't you). The
good news is, it lasted only for a minute before
the transformation began again. Suddenly my
vision returned, suddenly I had arms and hands
and legs. And the best part was, they were MY
arms and hands and legs.

"All right!" I shouted, jumping up and down
in excitement. Well, I tried jumping up and
down in excitement. But since coordination isn't
exactly my strength, I sort of stumbled and
kinda fell. The good news was, I didn't hit the
floor. Instead, I slammed into one of the nearby
bookcases. The bad news was, they don't make
bookcases like they used to.

Everyone looked up as the bookcase slowly

CREAKed

forward, tipping more and more until finally . . .

"Timber!"

it . . .

K-Thud

toppled into the next bookcase, which tilted forward until it . . .

K-Thud, K-Thud

fell into the next bookcase, which . . .

K-Thud, K-Thud, K-Thud

fell into the next one, which . . . well, I think you get the picture. Soon every bookcase in the room was falling into its neighbor. The entire library was going down like a giant set of dominoes.

I looked on, horrified. Horrified but also pleased that everything was returning to normal

. . . even my coordination. Yes sir, things were definitely returning to

K-Thud, K-Thud, K-Thud, K-Thud

normal.

Chapter 10

Wrapping Up

I was finally back to normal. You could see me, touch me, and do everything to me. Which means you could also put me in the back of the police car and call my parents on their business trip to tell them they had to come home immediately.

Call me a pessimist, but I figured Mom and Dad would be anything but thrilled over having to come home early. I also figured they'd be anything but thrilled over why they had to come home.

So, being the type who hates to die before he finishes writing his superhero stories, I called to the officer in the front seat of the squad car and asked, "Excuse me, sir? Could I borrow a pen and some paper?"

He looked back at me. "Why's that, kid?" He chuckled. "Planning to make out your last will and testament?"

(Obviously he knew my parents.)

"No, sir." I tried to grin. "I just want to kill some time by doing some writing."

"No problem," he said. "I'll find something. You're right. You're probably going to have a long wait."

"One can only hope," I mumbled, "one can only hope."

A minute or two later he produced a tablet and a pen . . . and immediately I went to work:

When we last left our hero, he was having all of his freckles rearranged by some reject robot from an old sci-fi series. But what of the notorious Neat Freak? Where is he? How can SuperSlob possibly have that final and obligatory (good thing you didn't put that dictionary away) showdown with so few pages left in this book? And more important—

Suddenly there is a very neat and well-behaved

FLASH

as Neat Freak appears in his perfectly tailored suit coat, pressed shirt, pressed slacks (and don't even ask about the crease his mother irons in his undershorts).

"Neat Freak!" our hero shouts. "How'd you get here so fast?"

"I AM UTILIZING VIRTUAL REALITY," the sinister non-slob says.

"IT IS MUCH NEATER TO DESTROY YOU THIS WAY WITH NONE OF THOSE BOTHERSOME BODY PARTS OR BLOOD TO CLEAN UP."

"But you can't win!" our hero shouts.

"AND WHY NOT?"

"Because I'm the hero in this story."

"YOU, THE HERO? I THINK NOT."

"It's true. Flip back to page 12 if you don't believe me."

"WHY WOULD OUR ESTEEMED WRITER MAKE A SLOB THE HERO?"

"I'm not sure, but I've got my ideas." Then, clearing his throat and spitting someplace gross (hey, hero or not, he's still a slob), he continues. "Enter 'Music School' into your virtual reality gizmo and let me show you."

With a heavy, though very carefully placed, sigh, Neat Freak nods, reaches for his controls, and

BEEP, BOP, BURP, BLEEP

enters the coordinates to the nearest music school. At least it's supposed to be a music school. But instead of music, everyone is playing one continuous note. One long, very boring, continuous note.

"WHAT IS WRONG WITH THEM?" Neat Freak shouts over the noise.

"THEY SOUND TERRIBLE!"

"Take a look at their sheet music," our hero yells. "It's the same note, over and over again, on every piece of paper in the entire school."

"YES, AND LOOK HOW NEAT AND TIDY IT APPEARS ON THE PAPER."

"That's my point. Neat and tidy isn't always a good thing. And it's not just with music. Enter 'Nearest Preschool' into your gizmo."

Neat Freak nods, and after the obligatory

BEEP, BOP, BURP, BLEEP,

the two find themselves in a preschool. But instead of neat, well-behaved children, everyone is crying.

"WHAT IS WRONG WITH THEM?" Neat Freak shouts.

"They're drawing dot-to-dot pictures," our hero explains.

"YES, I SEE. AND LOOK HOW NICELY I'VE ARRANGED ALL THEIR DOTS IN ONE NEAT AND VERY STRAIGHT ROW."

"And that's why they're crying. They can't draw any pictures of anything. All they can draw are long, straight lines."

"STRAIGHT LINES ARE NEAT AND TIDY."

"Yes, and they come in handy for things like painting stripes down freeways. But sometimes you need

things to be different. Like people. You can't have everybody wearing the same clothes, or having the same hair
or the same color skin."

"BUT YOU CANNOT HAVE EVERYONE
BEING A SLOB, EITHER."

"That's true," our hero says, coughing and spitting
again. "And there's probably some things in my act that
I need to clean up (though I can't imagine what). But
the point is, we're all individuals. And individuals need to
be . . . individuals."

"WOW, I THINK I SEE YOUR POINT!"

"Really?" our hero asks.

"NO, BUT IF YOU KEEP TALKING, I'M
AFRAID YOU'LL COUGH AND SPIT
SOME MORE."

"Oh, sorry. But I'd really like to show you some more
examples, if you don't mind."

"AS LONG AS I CAN SHOW YOU WHAT
WOULD HAPPEN IF EVERYBODY WAS
AS SLOPPY AS YOU."

"Deal," our hero says, reaching out his hand for a
shake.

"UH, YOU CAN'T SHAKE HANDS
WITH A VIRTUAL REALITY IMAGE."

"Oh, yeah, that's right."

And so the two stroll arm in arm toward the setting
sun—

"UH, YOU CAN'T STROLL ARM IN ARM

WITH VIRTUAL REALITY, EITHER."

"Oh, right, thanks." And so the two head off into the beautiful, warm sunset —

"UH, YOU CAN'T—"

"Got it." And so the two head off into the make-believe sunset, preparing to see how there is a place for both neatness—

"TOLD YOU SO."

—and not-such neatness—

"That's (cough, scratch-scratch, spit) right."

—in this old world.

I paused a moment, looking down at my ending. It wasn't great, but it was true. There was a place for both. As long as people didn't get too carried away in either direction.

"Hey, Wally!" Someone pounded on the police car window. "Wally."

I looked up to see Wall Street.

"One of your friends?" the officer asked from the front seat.

"Yes, sir. May I speak to her?"

"Sure, you're not under arrest or anything. We just need to keep you close 'til we hear from your parents."

"Thanks," I said as he got out and opened the door for me.

Wall Street was immediately beside me, checking out the inside of the car. "Cool," she said.

"Yeah," I mumbled. "Cool."

"So," she asked, "any idea what your parents are going to do to you when they get here?"

I shrugged. "The usual ground me for life, restrict me from TV 'til I'm forty-five, you know the routine."

"Yeah. Parents are funny that way. My mom make me return all the money to those people. Guess she figured they felt an invisible boy wasn't as interesting as a ghost."

"Sorry."

"That's okay," she said, lowering her voice. "Because I've got ourselves a brand-new gimmick."

Suddenly, my stomach was feeling a little queasy. "Wall Street, haven't we learned our lesson?"

"No, no, no, this is perfectly legit . . . well, almost."

My stomach felt no better.

"I've got three Hollywood studios lined up who want to do your story."

"*My* story?"

"Yeah, you know how the FBI forced you to become invisible so you could guard the

President and watch how he runs the country so
they could secretly install you as the next one?"

gurgle . . .

"Next what?" I asked.
"Next President, of course."

gurgle . . . gurgle . . .

"Wall Street—"
"I know some of the facts are a bit made up,
but who cares, just as long as—"
"Wall Street, selling a made-up story to them
and telling them it's true, that's just like cheating. And if there's one thing we've all learned
these past few days it's—"
"I know, I know, that if you cheat, don't get
caught."
"No, that's *not* what we learned! Wall
Street—"
"Wally, just listen to my plan—"
I tried to interrupt, but she kept right on
talking, explaining all the different ways we
could take shortcuts and make a ton of money
off the project.

Of course, I had to sit there and listen, but I wasn't buying it for one second. No sir. Because if there's one thing I learned, it's that cheating and taking shortcuts always wind up becoming the longest (not to mention most painful) way to get where you're going. Maybe it doesn't look that way at the beginning, but it's always that way at the

gurgle, gurgle, gurgle

end.

By the way, does anybody have another Rolaid?

You'll want to read them all.

THE INCREDIBLE WORLDS OF
WALLY McDOOGLE

#1—My Life As a Smashed Burrito with Extra Hot Sauce

Twelve-year-old Wally—the "Walking Disaster Area"—is forced to stand up to Camp Wahkah Wahkah's number one all-American bad guy. One hilarious mishap follows another until, fighting together for their very lives, Wally learns the need for even his worst enemy to receive Jesus Christ. (ISBN 0-8499-3402-8)

#2—My Life As Alien Monster Bait

"Hollyweird" comes to Middletown! Wally's a superstar! A movie company has chosen our hero to be eaten by their mechanical "Mutant from Mars"! It's a close race as to which will consume Wally first—the disaster-plagued special effects "monster" or his own out-of-control pride —until he learns the cost of true friendship and of God's command for humility. (ISBN 0-8499-3403-6)

#3—My Life As a Broken Bungee Cord

A hot-air balloon race! What could be more fun? Then again, we're talking about Wally McDoogle, the "Human Catastrophe." Calamity builds on calamity until, with his life on the line, Wally learns what it means to FULLY put his trust in God. (ISBN 0-8499-3404-4)

#4—My Life As Crocodile Junk Food

Wally visits missionary friends in the South American rain forest. Here he stumbles onto a whole new set of impossible predicaments . . . until he understands the need and joy of sharing Jesus Christ with others.
(ISBN 0-8499-3405-2)

#5—My Life As Dinosaur Dental Floss

It starts with a practical joke that snowballs into near disaster. Risking his life to protect his country, Wally is pursued by a SWAT team, bungling terrorists, photo-snapping tourists, Gary the Gorilla, and a TV news reporter. After prehistoric-size mishaps and a talk with the President, Wally learns that maybe honesty really is the best policy. (ISBN 0-8499-3537-7)

#6—My Life As a Torpedo Test Target

Wally uncovers the mysterious secrets of a sunken submarine. As dreams of fame and glory increase, so do the famous McDoogle mishaps. Besides hostile sea creatures, hostile pirates, and hostile Wally McDoogle clumsiness, there is the war against his own greed and selfishness. It isn't until Wally finds himself on a wild ride atop a misguided torpedo that he realizes the source of true greatness. (ISBN 0-8499-3538-5)

#7—My Life As a Human Hockey Puck

Look out . . . Wally McDoogle turns athlete! Jealousy and envy drive Wally from one hilarious calamity to another until, as the team's mascot, he learns humility while suddenly being thrown in to play goalie for the Middletown Super Chickens! (ISBN 0-8499-3601-2)

#8—My Life As an Afterthought Astronaut

"Just 'cause I didn't follow the rules doesn't make it my fault that the Space Shuttle almost crashed. Well, okay, maybe it was sort of my fault. But not the part when Pilot O'Brien was spacewalking and I accidentally knocked him halfway to Jupiter . . ." So begins another hilarious Wally McDoogle MISadventure as our boy blunder stows aboard the Space Shuttle and learns the importance of: Obeying the Rules!
(ISBN 0-8499-3602-0)

#9—My Life As Reindeer Road Kill

Santa on an out-of-control four wheeler? Electrical Rudolph on the rampage? Nothing unusual, just Wally McDoogle doing some last-minute Christmas shopping . . . FOR GOD! Our boy blunder dreams that an angel has invited him to a birthday party for Jesus. Chaos and comedy follow as he turns the town upside down looking for the perfect gift, until he finally bumbles his way into the real reason for the Season. (ISBN 0-8499-3866-X)

#10—My Life As a Toasted Time Traveler

Wally travels back from the future to warn himself of an upcoming accident. But before he knows it, there are more Wallys running around than even Wally himself can handle. Catastrophes reach an all-time high as Wally tries to out-think God and rewrite history. (ISBN 0-8499-3867-8)

#11—My Life As Polluted Pond Scum

This laugh-filled Wally disaster includes: a monster lurking in the depths of a mysterious lake . . . a glowing figure with powers to summon the creature to the shore . . . and one Wally McDoogle, who reluctantly stumbles upon the truth. Wally's entire town is in danger. He must race against the clock and his own fears and learn to trust God before he has any chance of saving the day. (ISBN 0-8499-3875-9)

#12—My Life As a Bigfoot Breath Mint

Wally gets his big break to star with his uncle Max in the famous Fantasmo World stunt show. Unlike his father, whom Wally secretly suspects to be a major loser, Uncle Max is everything Wally longs to be . . . or so it appears. But Wally soon discovers the truth and learns who the real hero is in his life. (ISBN 0-8499-3876-7)

#13—My Life As a Blundering Ballerina

Wally agrees to switch places with Wall Street. Everyone is in on the act as the two try to survive seventy-two hours in each other's shoes and learn the importance of respecting other people. (ISBN 0-8499-4022-2)

#14—My Life As a Screaming Skydiver

Master of mayhem Wally turns a game of laser tag into international espionage. From the Swiss Alps to the African plains, Agent 00½th bumblingly employs such top-secret gizmos as rocket-powered toilet paper, exploding dental floss, and the ever-popular transformer tacos to stop the dreaded and super secret . . . Giggle Gun. (ISBN 0-8499-4023-0)

#15—My Life As a Human Hairball

When Wally and Wall Street visit a local laboratory, they are accidentally miniaturized and swallowed by some unknown stranger. It is a race against the clock as they fly through various parts of the body in a desperate search for a way out while learning how wonderfully we're made. (ISBN 0-8499-4024-9)

#16—My Life As a Walrus Whoopee Cushion

Wally and his buddies, Opera and Wall Street, win the Gazillion Dollar Lotto! Everything is great, until they realize they lost the ticket at the zoo! Add some bungling bad guys, a zoo break-in, the release of all the animals, a SWAT team or two . . . and you have the usual McDoogle mayhem as Wally learns the dangers of greed. (ISBN 0-8499-4025-7)

#17—My Life As a Mixed-Up Millennium Bug

When Wally accidentally fries the circuits of Ol' Betsy, his beloved laptop computer, suddenly whatever he types turns into reality! At 11:59, New Year's Eve, Wally tries retyping the truth into his computer—which shorts out every other computer in the world. By midnight, the entire universe has credited Wally's mishap to the MILLENNIUM BUG! Panic, chaos, and hilarity start the new century, thanks to our beloved boy blunder. (ISBN 0-8499-4026-5)

#18—My Life As a Beat-Up Basketball Backboard

Ricko Slicko's Advertising Agency claims that they can turn the dorkiest human in the world into the most popu-lar. And who better to prove this than our boy blunder, Wally McDoogle! Soon he has his own TV series and fans wearing glasses just like his. But when he tries to be a star athlete for his school basketball team, Wally finally learns that being popular isn't all it's cut out to be. (ISBN 0-8499-4027-3)

#19—*My Life As a Cowboy Cowpie*

Once again our part-time hero and full-time walking disaster area finds himself smack dab in another misadventure. This time it's full of dude-ranch disasters, bungling broncobusters, and the world's biggest cow—well, let's just say it's not a pretty picture (or a pleasant-smelling one). Through it all, Wally learns the dangers of seeking revenge. (ISBN 0-8499-5990-X)

Would You Like To Interview

Bill Myers
In Your Classroom?

If your class has access to
a speaker phone, you can interview
Bill Myers, author of The Incredible
Worlds of Wally McDoogle series,
which has sold over 1 million copies.
You'll be able to ask him about his
life as a writer and how he created
the famous boy blunder.

It's Fun!
It's Easy!
It's Educational!

For information, just have your
teacher e-mail us at
Tommy Nelson® and ask for details!
E-mail: prdept@tommynelson.com